# *Is It Them or Is It Me?*

Susan Haven

# *Is It Them or Is It Me?*

G. P. Putnam's Sons, New York

## Acknowledgments

I would like to thank my editor, Anne O'Connell, whose suggestions and support were so helpful; my husband, Mark, and my son, Paul, whose poem about a certain less than inspiring teacher inspired this book.

A special thanks goes to Paula Danziger without whose help and encouragement this book would never have been completed.

---

Copyright © 1990 by Susan Haven
G. P. Putnam's Sons, a division of The Putnam & Grosset Book Group, 200 Madison Avenue, New York, NY 10016.
Published simultaneously in Canada.
Printed in the United States of America.
Book design by Gunta Alexander.
Library of Congress Cataloging in Publication Data
Haven, Susan Perkis.
Is it them or is it me?
Summary: Molly's first weeks in high school provide her with some unforgettable experiences with new friends, new teachers, and a crisis at home.
[1. High schools—Fiction. 2. Schools—Fiction.
3. Friendship—Fiction. 4. Family problems—Fiction]
I. Title.  PZ7.H299No  1990   [Fic]   89-24304
ISBN 0-399-21916-1

10  9  8  7  6  5  4  3  2  1

First Impression

*To my brother,*
*whose wristburns made this book possible*
*With love*

# Chapter 1

"Down, Princess, please," I say to the Marantzes' giant dalmatian as I open the screen door.

"Princess, I mean it. I beg you."

Just as I'm stretching my neck to free my nose, there is the welcome thud of running Reebok sneakers.

"Hiii!" Kathy pulls Princess off me and shakes a finger at her. "No!"

The dog immediately lies down and looks guilty.

My friend grins. "You just have to be firm, Molly. Come on in."

Following her into the Marantzes' kitchen, I try to see how ready Kathy is. She's dressed. Her hair is done. But she's still munching on an English muffin. Slowly.

"C'mon, Kathy. Hurry. We don't want to be late."

"We don't?" She swallows the last bite.

"No, we don't." Then, to reassure her, I add, "You look great!"

She does. She's wearing black stirrup pants, a tight V-neck purple top and two sets of earrings on each ear—gold hearts and porcelain danglies. Pretty sexy.

She runs her fingers through her wild, strawberry blond hair. "You look great too, Molly."

"Thanks."

I hope so. I've got on a gray and black long rayon skirt, a white T-shirt that says on the back "I'm leaving now. I've had just about enough" and a long black cardigan. I wear the cardigan because it goes with my outfit, not because I have a great figure to hide.

So far, unfortunately, I'm still built like a Tootsie Pop. Tall and skinny.

But I'm optimistic. My mom has a great figure, and my Grandmother Irma has a chest like the Swiss Alps.

I'm hoping to be a late bloomer.

Kathy holds her stomach. "I'm so nervous."

"Me too. I wish we were both going to Bryan, but, at least we can walk to school together," I say. "You're only a block from me."

Kathy sticks out her tongue and rolls her eyes like she's about to faint.

Today's the first day of high school for both of us, but for the first time in our lives, Kathy Marantz, my best friend since second grade, and I are going to different schools. I'm going to William Jennings Bryan, the best public high school in Verona, Long Island. But Kathy's going to St. Bartholomew's Parish School, a very ritzy private academy. Her dad went there, and so did her grandfather. Now she's got to go, and she's not happy about it.

I can't blame her. All the kids in our development call it St. Muffy's. It's snob city. And one thing Kathy isn't is a snob.

I grin. "C'mon, Kathy. Honest, it's going to be okay."

"Easy for you to say. You'll be at a normal school."

I shrug. But she's right.

"Morning, Molly!" Mrs. Marantz, Kathy's mother, walks over. She's putting on her suit jacket and surveying the counters. "Did anybody see my briefcase?"

Kathy shakes her head, then glares back at her mother. I think she's angry at everybody for making her go to St. Muffy's.

"There it is." Mrs. Marantz gives her daughter a hug. "You know it's my first day of school too, honey. I'm just as nervous."

After Mr. and Mrs. Marantz got divorced, Mrs. Marantz went back to school. Now she's a professor of psychology at Verona Junior College. She's smart and nice. Turning to me, she says, "You know, Molly, Bryan is my alma mater. I know you'll love it. A kid as nice as you . . ."

"Thanks. I hope so." I turn to my friend.

"Come on, Kathy, I have to be in my homeroom in twenty minutes."

"Okay, okay. . ." She takes a deep breath, puts on her leather jacket, throws a kiss to her two parakeets, four gerbils and three guinea pigs and we head for the door.

We walk to school along the bay.

Verona is on a little inlet which runs into Long Island Sound. It's very pretty and there are sailboats and motorboats bobbing and bouncing on the water.

"Pretty, isn't it?" I say.

"Eh. It's polluted," Kathy responds. "This bay will probably be legally dead in a few years."

I can't help it. I burst out laughing at her bad mood.

Which makes Kathy laugh because I sound like a goose. I kind of inhale and honk at the same time.

I hate my laughs. I giggle. I even snort sometimes. I'm so unsophisticated. So uncool. So unhigh school.

I wish I could develop a mature, cool laugh by the time I get to Bryan.

I wish I could mature altogether by the time I get to Bryan.

Kathy turns to me. "You know, my dad introduced me to a kid at his tennis club who's going to St. Bartholomew's," she mutters. "You know what his name is? Henderson Willoughby. The Fourth. You know what his nickname is? Henny! Yuk."

I start to laugh again but stop myself. "Look," I

say slowly and calmly. "I won't know that many kids at Bryan either. There are ten junior high schools besides Whitman that send kids there. I'm scared too."

She nods. "But they're all regular kids. Plus, your own brother's a junior."

I nod. "Yeah. But he made me promise not to go near him."

I hate my brother Billy.

It's not just that he's mean to me, or that he tortures me or that he hates me.

No. I think that's what it is.

For two years Billy's been at William Jennings Bryan while I was still at Walt Whitman Junior High. Those were great years.

Kathy grins. "You make fun of Billy. But you're lucky. I wish I had a brother or a sister to love."

"So do I." And I mean it.

Actually, Kathy is almost like a sister to me. We look different but we have a lot in common too. We both love to talk. About people. Or the news. Or the meaning of life. Just yesterday, we had a long discussion about what either of us would do if an ugly boy asked us for a date and we said yes, but then a gorgeous hunk asked us out the next day.

I said I'd keep the date with the dweeb. It was the right thing to do. But Kathy asked how I knew the dweeb wouldn't drop me if a gorgeous girl made eyes at him.

Kathy's a realist. She says I'm an optimist.

Which is kind of half true. I'm optimistic about

11

the future. But I worry about everything in the present.

Anyway, so far, neither of us have a real honest to goodness boyfriend. But I'm ready.

I'm so ready.

We stop at the corner of Ramona Avenue. To the left is St. Bart's, to the right is Bryan.

"This is it," I say gently.

Her eyes look a little teary.

I grip her shoulders. "Kathy, don't worry. I don't care who those rich kids are. I don't care how confident, how famous their parents, how snotty, how . . ." I stop in midsentence. I think I'm using the wrong approach. "Let me put it another way. High school only lasts four years. Someday, when we're both married, with three kids each, and I run into you at the mall, we'll look back at this day and laugh."

When either of us feels lousy, this technique usually helps. "Tell me more," Kathy says.

I think fast. "Well, it'll be ten years from now. We won't have seen each other for a while. You'll be running to your car where the handsomest husband in America—except for mine—will be sitting in the front seat, waiting. Your adorable triplets will be asleep in the backseat. You'll drop some packages in his lap, then kiss him good-bye because you have to rush over to the Kathy Marantz Veterinary Clinic where you're needed to save the life of a sick stallion. For which you'll eventually win the Nobel Prize."

She grins. "And then . . ."

12

"And then we'll see each other and hug. And I'll say, 'Remember the first day of high school?' And you'll say, 'Vaguely . . .'"

"And what are you doing there?"

I rub my hands together and think. "Uh . . . I'll probably be there doing a story for CBS news on the high cost of consumer goods. I'll call it 'Shame of the Malls.'"

"Didn't you do a story at Whitman on graffiti? Didn't you call that 'Shame of Our Halls'?"

I pretend to be annoyed. "Hey—gimme a break. I'm late."

"Sorry." Kathy laughs. "I feel better. I really do. Speaking of malls, are we going Friday after school?"

"For sure. Now, call me tonight no matter what, okay?"

"Right."

And, patting her shoulder as a good-bye, I turn and begin to run. I've got three minutes to get to my homeroom class.

William Jennings Bryan High School—here I come!

# Chapter 2

Bryan is built like a castle, with two concrete towers in front, and a shorter brick building that squares around a little green campus. It's majestic, it's heroic, and it's big.

It's a fairy tale come true.

I walk into the entrance. It's also very dark because the halls are olive green, the floors are black and not all the fluorescent lights seem to be working.

Kids are rushing everywhere. Bryan has over three thousand of them.

A boy wearing a "Welcome to Bryan!" button stops me.

"Freshman?" he asks.

"Yes," I answer. I wonder how he can tell.

"Do you have the postcard with your official classroom?"

I wrinkle my nose. "Gee, I forgot it. But I know my room is 253."

14

"No good. You need the card for me to let you in."

My stomach drops. "Oh, gosh. What should I do?"

More kids are rushing by me, right and left. They're so big, so tall, so old.

The boy shrugs. "Well," he says in a drawl. "I'll let you go—even though I shouldn't . . ."

"Oh thanks!" I answer gratefully.

He thrusts a piece of paper toward me. "You better buy a copy of the BSG, though."

"Huh?"

"The Bryan Student Guide. It's put out by the WBSC. The William Bryan Student Council. It'll keep you out of trouble. It's fifty cents and the money goes to the student council."

"Sure. Sure." Reaching into my pocket, I pull out fifty cents and hand it over.

The BSG. The WBSC. It's all so exciting.

I rush up to the second floor. As I head for Room 253, it seems like a million kids are coming toward me.

"Move!" A kid pushes me. Then another.

I paste myself against the wall, then let about a hundred more kids pass before I move again.

One of them is Derek Anderson who went to Whitman with me. He was the belching king of eighth grade.

He's halfway down the hall when he turns around and walks back.

"Hey, Molly Snyder, I thought that was you," he smiles and belches a quick short belch that sounds

15

like a cork popping. "Watch it. The halls here are one way since they go completely around the square. It's like a stampede if you're going the wrong way."

"I see that."

I'm glad my back's to the wall. Derek was also the bra snapping king at Whitman.

But I can't help noticing that he looks different since the summer. He's taller. He grew an Adam's apple. And his straight blond hair hangs over blue eyes which are bigger than I remember.

Still, moving away from the wall, I keep the front of my body facing him.

Derek just smiles and asks if I've gotten my program yet.

I shake my head. "I'm on my way . . ."

"My brother Charlie is a senior and he's going to analyze mine for me. If you get yours in time, come on down to the auditorium. That's where we'll be."

"Gee . . . thanks, Derek."

Another boy stops beside us.

"Hey, Michael." Derek jabs him in the shoulder.

"Hey, Derek. How's it going?" The boy has a halo of short sandy hair and exudes confidence. He also has a deep mellow voice, like a tv newsman.

Derek introduces us. "Michael Dukes—this is Molly Snyder."

Michael stares at me with eyes that would defrost my mom's refrigerator.

I want to stand and stare back at him for a couple of years, but all I do is nod, mumble "I gotta go" and back away.

When it comes to boys, I'm such a chicken.

16

When I reach my homeroom, it's almost as mobbed as the halls. I slip into a backseat just as the door closes and a male teacher walks in.

"Hello, class. My name is Mr. Werbell." He turns around and writes the name in enormous letters on the board. "That's Werbell. With the accent on the *bell*. Welcome to Bryan High School." He smiles broadly at all of us. "Now, as your name is called, come and pick up your program."

He takes out a stack of cards, removes a rubber band and continues.

"If you have a question about your program, you may line up to the left of my desk to discuss it. If you have a legitimate cause for complaint, you may go down to the program office and get on line there."

Mr. Werbell looks around, his hand over his eyebrows, surveying the class, and then smiles.

"I might mention that I just came from the program office. The line is slightly longer than the line for the Christmas show at Radio City Music Hall. However, don't be discouraged. I'm sure that if you are determined to make a change, you will eventually get to the head of the line. A student of mine from last spring waited patiently, and sure enough, he just got to the head of the line."

He chuckles again. "I'm kidding." He looks around again. "Freshmen . . ." he says. "So sweet . . ." Then he adds, "If you have no problems, you may leave for the Freshman Orientation in the auditorium. There you will be welcomed, IDed and fingerprinted."

I feel half scared by Mr. Werbell, and half relaxed. He looks like a nice guy. He's tall and chubby and he's wearing a Mets baseball cap. He's a real high school teacher, a little dorky but in a very grown-up way.

Looking down at the program cards, he starts reading. "Bergof, Cruz, Edwards . . ." Kids come forward as he puts each card on his desk. "Frick, Henderson, Kiner . . ."

I look them over. I don't know anybody. Not a single person in the whole room.

After reading a few more names, Mr. Werbell interrupts himself again. "If you do leave early, remember. Beware of upperclassmen. Some will try to sell you pool passes. We have no pool. And don't let them charge you for school guidebooks. They're free at every entrance and staircase."

I'm going to get that kid.

"Paterson, Podres, Robinson, Snyder . . ."

I rush up to look for my card on the desk.

As I reach for it, Mr. Werbell gestures to me.

"Are you any relation to Billy Snyder?"

I nod. "He's my brother."

"Tsk tsk tsk." he says. "He was in my chemistry lab. Are you anything like him?"

I shake my head vigorously.

"Good."

I nod and go back to my seat.

Besides being mean, my brother is a terrible student. He's gorgeous, and popular, and he's on the Bryan track team, but he's always flunking courses

18

and playing hooky and my father is always yelling at him. They don't get along at all.

I'm nothing like Billy. I work like a dog.

I have no choice. My dad has his heart set on me going to a top college.

I want to do well at Bryan, but just thinking about all the A's I'll need gives me a stomachache.

I walk back to my desk and study my program.

It seems to be okay. All the right subjects are listed. There's only one bad thing. I have lunch first period, at 8:30 in the morning.

But getting on that line will take forever since it's already starting to reach the hall.

Besides, I'd rather get to the auditorium and talk to Derek's brother. And Derek.

Ducking out the backdoor, I lower my head and wiggle through a thinner horde of kids. I ask a tall boy with glasses how to get to the auditorium.

"All the way to your left, down the stairs, across the overpass, and down the stairs again."

I can't find the overpass so I stop another kid and ask again. "All the way to your right, up three flights, and to your left."

I ignore that advice and ask a girl. She sends me to the boiler room.

I'm starting to get a tiny bit upset when I finally spot the word "Auditorium" on the wall. Next to it is an "Up" arrow. I bound up the stairs.

Derek, Michael and Charlie are hanging out beside the big doors.

"Hi," I say shyly.

Derek grins. "Charlie, you know Molly Snyder, Billy Snyder's sister . . . they live in Home Acres. . . . Could you look at her program?"

Charlie looks me over. He's about two feet taller than Derek and twice as broad. "Sure, why not."

Taking the card from my hesitant hands, he looks it over carefully. "Uh hummm. Not bad, excellent, good, not bad, good, good . . . uh ohhh . . ."

"Uh oh? What? Tell me. . ." I say nervously.

Two jocks with Bryan jackets pass and Charlie waves to them.

They are so cool.

I can't wait until I start waving to kids in the halls.

Charlie looks down at my card again. "You want to hear the good news first?" he asks me.

"Sure." As I try to smile cheerfully, Charlie leans his elbow against the wall and begins talking to me on a slant. I slant my head to listen.

"Well, first of all, you're lucky. You have Mrs. Brown for health. She's ninety years old."

"That's good?"

"Definitely. She falls asleep within fifteen minutes. During those fifteen minutes, she'll tell you everything you ever wanted to know about adolescence in the nineteenth century. But she's nice."

I laugh.

He continues. "You have Medina for English." He gestures to Michael and Derek. "You're with them. She's the best teacher in the school and adviser to the school newspaper."

"Great!" I say. "Because I'm trying out for the *Bugle*."

Derek pats me on the back. "Molly's a great reporter," he says to Michael. To me, he adds, "I'm trying out for the *Bugle*'s photography squad. And Michael was editor of the Glenwood High *Gazette*."

Michael takes a pen from his ear. "Yeah. But you know there's a *Bugle* sign-up sheet in the auditorium. And I must have been the fiftieth name . . ." He sighs. "Somebody told me to come up with article ideas before the first meeting. The key is getting a good first tryout assignment."

I nod at him, and stare at his slightly cauliflower ears. On Michael, they look sexy.

Charlie snaps his fingers at us. "I don't have all day to babysit, guys. Let's go." He opens a pack of gum, and sticks all five pieces in his mouth, one by one.

"Okay." There are liquid noises in between his sentences. "Now let's see. For biology, you have Walsh. That's also good. He can't teach but he gives every pretty girl a ninety."

"Ah hah." I say that casually, but being called pretty fills my heart with gratitude.

Charlie looks up from the card. "You also have Mrs. Caponata for Latin. She's from Italy and speaks very little English, so she forgets and teaches Latin in Italian." The gum in his mouth cracks. "You'll probably need a tutor."

My stomach dives. "Gee," I ask nervously, "Is that why you said 'uh oh'?"

He laughs at me. "Are you kidding? I call her

21

good. She marks on a curve." He sucks in air through his teeth and chews for a few silent seconds as he scans my card again. "You also have Bloom." He studies my face. "But you look smart. If you're good at math you can pretty much learn by yourself. So, even though she's had two nervous breakdowns, I don't want to worry you unnecessarily."

I'm starting to hyperventilate. "Oh. Gee. Then, she was the uh oh?"

Charlie shakes his head sadly. "I'm afraid not, Molly." He gestures toward Derek and Michael. "You might as well join them. You're all in the same boat. Stand on line at the program office. Come up with something. Anything. But get out of this guy's class. I say this because I have great respect for human life, even freshman human life." He shrugs. "Although . . . it's probably hopeless. If they let one kid out, everybody'd try . . ."

Now I've stopped breathing altogether.

Charlie hands back my program card as two more friends pass. "Would you believe it, the poor devils," he calls to them. "All three of them."

"What?" I ask nervously. "What could be so terrible?"

His eyes meet each of ours, then rest on mine. "Molly, you have Henry Frack for history. He doesn't teach, he yells, and he's singlehandedly responsible for keeping summer school full. We like to call him Frack the Hack. A man who makes the Marquis de Sade seem like a Ken doll." Cracking his gum one more time, Charlie sticks out his hand to shake mine. "But welcome to Bryan."

22

# Chapter 3

As soon as I get home, I try to call Kathy. No answer.

Then I spend the next half hour trying to do two important things: come up with ideas for my *Bugle* tryout and go to the bathroom.

But it's hard to come up with Pulitzer Prize articles with your legs crossed. And I can't get into the bathroom because my brother's been in there forever.

My parents ought to rent out Billy's room. Half his life is spent in the john. When he takes a bath, he sometimes brings in stereo speakers and a chocolate layer cake.

I uncross my legs, walk into the hall, peek under the bottom crack of the bathroom door and see his smog gray Reebok sneakers. I can hear the faint sound of rock music coming from his Walkman stereo.

"Billy, are you coming out this year or what?"

No answer.

I walk back to my desk, pick up my pen and sit down. But the only idea I have for an article is on the human kidney. I get up again, head for the kitchen and reread my mother's note.

Kids:
Got home from the office but I had a
doctor's appointment. Be back by six.
Molly, could you put on the rice.
Meanwhile—there's cheese and/or raw
vegetables for snacks. Homemade chocolate
cream pie is FOR DINNER.
XXXXXXXXXX Love, Mom
P.S. DON'T FIGHT!
THIS MEANS BOTH OF YOU!
P.P.S. How was school? I hope great!

I open the refrigerator door and stare at the chocolate cream pie. Scooping some whipped cream off the pie with a carrot stick, I even out the topping so my mother won't notice, and yell again.

"Billy! Come out! Your room's on fire!"

Nothing.

Turning on the tap, I begin to fill a pot with water. But running the water reminds me of my problem.

"Billy, pullease come out!"

I walk to the bathroom and bang against the door once again.

This time, I pound so hard that it creaks open.

Accidentally, I peek inside.

And I can't believe it! No Billy!

24

The light is on, the seat is up, but instead of my brother, there are only his two sneakers stuffed with socks standing at attention in front of the toilet. His Walkman is blaring beside them.

On the wall is a sheet of paper. I rip it down and read:

Ha ha Molly. Are you dumb!
Your loving brother, Billy

I could kill him. I could grab his sixteen-year-old face right then and there and pluck out his nose hairs one by one.

A hand taps my shoulder and I pivot around. It's him.

"Hi!" he says, chuckling happily.

So I hit him over the head with the rice pot. Hard.

"Owwww," Billy grabs his scalp with two hands as I scream, "I'll kill you," and try to find another opening to his brains.

Just then, the screen door opens and my mom comes up behind us.

My brother starts moaning again, superloudly.

"What's going on here?" she asks as I lower the pot behind my back.

Billy looks at my mother and winces again. "The dweeb hit me with a pot. I think I have a concussion."

My teeth are gritted. My eyes are bulging. "Mom, he locked me out of the bathroom for an hour!"

As the anger rises again, so does the rice pot and my mom grabs it.

"C'mon you two! Stop this!" She sneezes.

Billy smiles sweetly at her. "How was the doctor, Mom? I was a little worried about you."

He gives her one of his dimpled smiles. The kind that lights up his big blue eyes.

He definitely is a handsome slimeball.

This is very embarrassing to admit, but my brother is prettier than I am.

My mom blows her nose, and wakes me up. "The doctor's fine, Billy. Now, Molly, are you serious? Did he . . ."

When I put the note in my mom's open hand, she reads it and then scowls at Billy. "You're grounded Saturday, young man. This is not funny."

Billy's lip curls into a snarl, his eyes glare at me.

I glare right back, mutter, "If you ask me you got off easy. You deserve life imprisonment," and slide between them into the john.

But as I pee, I listen carefully to the two of them. With my charming brother, punishment is never a sure thing.

"Mom," Billy begins. "I don't mind being grounded. It's just that Saturday, Dana Brown, the most beautiful girl in the junior class, personally asked me to come to a party. It means a lot to me."

"Really?" my mom answers gently.

"I like Dana a lot . . . in a very . . . a lot way."

"I see." My mother hesitates.

Hesitation is my brother's ally.

"Well . . . okay, Billy. I'll change it to Friday. But that's it!"

I flush quickly and open the door.

"Mom, he's home anyway this Friday!" I holler. "Remember, I almost lost a kidney!"

She hands me back the pot. "You, young lady, make the rice." Then she shakes her head at Billy again. "And you're grounded *next* Saturday. That's final!"

Billy nods and hugs her, smirking at me behind her back as I head for the kitchen.

By next Saturday my mom might forget.

I might even forget.

Life just isn't fair. My brother's been pulling these stunts since I was born and he always gets away with them because he's so damn cute.

While I'm stirring the rice, my mom walks up beside me.

"Hiyyy there!" she pipes cheerfully.

I give her my sourest look.

She nods. "C'mon, honey, it was just a joke. You know, deep down inside, Billy loves you."

"Oh yeah? You know what Aunt Annie told me last night on the phone? That when I came home from the hospital—my second day of life—she caught him near the bassinet giving me my first wristburn with a baby bracelet. He's no good. Face it, he's a wretch, Mom . . ."

She puts her arm around me and laughs. "Be generous, Molly. You know what I'm talking about."

I nod. She means that Billy's always in trouble. He's "insecure." He's got "problems."

27

She thinks because I'm easy, I'm the lucky one.

I don't think so. I think it's Billy who has it easy.

All he worries about is which girls in the junior class have a crush on him.

They don't put any pressure on him to get A's. Or to take Latin. Or to get into a good college.

They're just praying he'll graduate from high school before he's eligible for social security.

It's going to be a close call.

She kisses me again. "So, how was your first day?"

"Okay . . . I think." Then I tell her everything and she listens sympathetically.

"I remember my first day of high school. It's tough."

"Really? Did you get lost in the boiler room?"

She grins. "No. But I was just as scared and shy."

I look at her skeptically. My mom is always telling me how scared she was, and how unconfident she was about everything, but it's hard to believe. She seems so perfect now. She's beautiful and she's a vice-president of creative development at the Carter Toy Company.

I ask her more about her day because she seems a little sad too.

Studying the rice, she sighs. "I . . . I was a little disappointed about a toy I was working on . . . Halley Hiccough."

"Mom, you know the toy business has its ups and downs. You always tell me that."

She smiles. "You're so sweet. Actually, I'm more

28

upset that my boss wants me to develop a new idea. Decorator diapers for dolls." She wrinkles her nose. "Maybe I'll go back to college. Learn something serious. Is astrophysics hard?"

We both laugh and when I start to honk, she hugs me.

My mom loves my laugh. And my enthusiasm. She doesn't understand how dorky it is at my age. She doesn't understand that being sweet is a pain.

"When's the first newspaper meeting?" she asks.

"Next Monday."

"Good. Because guess what I bought?" She pulls out a tan raincoat from the shopping bag that's standing near the door.

"An English Fog. You'll look just like a reporter. And I got it on sale."

"Slightly imperfect?" I ask.

She wrinkles her nose. "Just slightly."

Sometimes my mom gets great bargains. Sometimes I wind up with belts that have no holes or sweaters that reach my toes.

"Try it on," she says, enthusiastically.

I do. I have to admit that it looks great.

"It's fabulous," she says. "Very stylish. It's even got Velcro snaps down the front to keep you warm."

"Thanks, Mom."

"And you look beautiful in it. As usual."

Mother love is so blind.

Just then the phone rings. My mom picks it up. It's Kathy. At last.

"Hi, Molly!" she bursts out as soon as I put the

receiver to my ear and stretch the cord around a corner for some privacy. "How'd it go at Bryan?"

"Okay . . . fair. How was St. Muffy's . . . I mean St. Bart's?"

"You won't believe this. But it was great!"

"Really?" I can't help it—I'm a little surprised. A little—uneasy. But I ask her to tell me more.

"It's small. And the teachers are so nice. And . . ."

She pauses.

"And . . . what?" I say nervously.

"And I met a boy!"

I knew it.

She continues. "He's president of the Junior Class. I sat at his table for lunch. And he drove me home. Nick Robinson. Is that the greatest name or what!"

"Wow," I manage to say. "That's great, Kathy."

"You were so right about St. Bart's. Wait 'til you meet Nick. He is so adorable!"

"That's great."

I take a deep breath. I don't think I can say "that's great" one more time.

"So," Kathy asks. "Why is Bryan not great?"

I tell her the truth. "It's big. And I got lost. And my teachers sound terrible . . . and I have lunch at dawn . . ."

"Gee, that's too bad. Especially since . . ." She stops.

"What?"

"Well . . ." She hesitates. "I know that we planned on walking to school together every morning. But Nick asked to pick me up in his car tomorrow. And I was wondering if you'd mind."

"Me? Mind?" I say. "Of course not. How could you not ride in a boy's car? I understand."

"Honest?" she asks.

"Sure." I half mean it too.

"Thanks. But we'll go to the mall on Friday, okay?"

"Definitely!" Winding the cord around and around my body, I add, "Actually, I need to get to the mall. Because I did talk to two boys at Bryan and . . ."

"Gotta go!" Suddenly, the phone clicks, and then a dial tone buzzes in my ear.

Kathy hung up on me.

As I put down the receiver, I keep my hand on it, frowning.

Maybe someday when I love school, when I make the newspaper, when I have friends, when I fall in love, I'll look back on this first day and laugh. Just like I told Kathy.

I force myself to smile.

But it doesn't quite work.

When you're not really feeling it, smiling makes your face hurt.

# Chapter 4

On the other hand, when you do feel like it, smiling is great.

And right now I feel like it because it's Friday afternoon at WJB High.

All I have to do is get through history and then I can head for Kathy's house. And then the mall.

Frack's sitting at his desk working on some papers and seems to be in no hurry to acknowledge our existence. So I take out my looseleaf and doodle a note to myself which reads "Latin is Greek to me," and think about my first full week at Bryan.

It's been mixed.

The hardest part is still not knowing anybody. If a freshman girl even looks at me, I smile back, but I haven't had one actual conversation. One girl, Laura Samuels, is in three of my classes. We keep nodding to each other, but I think she's even shyer than I am.

When I spoke to Kathy on the phone this week, I told her about my teachers and the newspaper tryouts. But I was embarrassed to say I was lonely. I'm a teenager. I'm supposed to be suffering from peer pressure and I don't have any peers yet.

Actually, so far the best thing about Bryan is the teachers. Except for Frack.

Ms. Medina's English class is great. She's interesting and she really listens to kids.

Maybe Mrs. Bloom is crazy, but she's also very funny. Every time somebody doesn't listen to her, she says, "You remind me of my first husband." And every time you give a right answer she says, "Supa!" We already had a class pool counting the number of "Supas!" she said for the week and I won a buck.

Even Mrs. Caponata is hard but fair. I got a 44 on my first Latin quiz, but she promised she would either drop one grade or add up our two lowest grades. So if I get a 46 on the next, I'll have a ninety average.

But then there's Frack.

Charlie was right. He's awful. Half the time he doesn't teach, just distributes handouts. It's so boring, it's hard not to talk or fidget. Then he gives detentions or zeros, or lectures us about what's wrong with our class, or our school, or our whole generation.

Uh oh. He's running his hand over his bald eagle head. He usually does that before standing up.

He's standing.

Please be nice, Mr. Frack.

And if you can't be nice, please, please don't call on me.

He's heading for the closet. His back is toward us, but I can see he's grabbing a stack of three by five yellow paper.

Walking from row to row, he begins passing them out.

A surprise quiz. Damn.

There's murmuring all around me.

"No talking. This is a quiz." Frack brushes his scalp again. "Ready? First question."

A few kids mumble "wait, wait," because half of us haven't gotten paper yet, but Frack plows ahead. "Question number one. What is the exact date of the Boston Tea Party? Question number two. What was the name of the ship in Boston Harbor? Question three." He takes a deep breath just as I receive my yellow paper. I can't even remember the first question anymore. I lean over and ask Karen Aaron, Frack's favorite student.

She's suddenly deaf.

I turn to the kid on my right, Jason "Inky" Grant, who went to Whitman with me. In just three days of school, he already has ink on his writing fingers, his shirt pocket, and his brand new looseleaf. By the last day of school, he could be completely blue. But he's a good guy.

"Jason? What's the first question?" I whisper.

He whispers back. "The date of the Boston Tea Party."

"Right . . . thanks." Frack glares over at us and I slide down in my seat.

I think hard about the first question, but I don't know the answer.

34

Not only that, now I've forgotten the second question.

My heart is pounding, but I raise my hand.

Frack stares right through me for a second, but then says, "Yes?"

"Could you repeat the second question?"

He shakes his head. "I don't repeat. Question number three. What is the name of the American Revolutionary leader who planned the Boston Tea Party?"

Thank goodness. I know that one from fourth grade. Samuel Adams. I write it down.

Frack walks down the third row, staring at every desk he passes. When he reaches the back, he leans against the blackboard and asks us the last question. "Finally, for half your grade, who was X. R. Parker?"

X. R. Parker? The only Parker I know lives down the block from us. It can't be him. I read the whole chapter last night, answered all the questions, and I never heard of X. R. Parker.

It looks like I'm going to get a twelve and a half on the first history quiz.

"Time's up," Frack barks as he strides back up to the front of the room. "Pens down. Pass your papers. No dawdling."

Frack is so stern, so scary that my stomach knots. He's giving me what my grandma calls a condition.

I shudder as the stack of test papers comes forward from the girl behind me and I have to add my failing sheet to the pile.

I did the homework so carefully. For nothing.

Just as Frack is collecting the last of the tests at

the front of each row, Inky raises his hand. "Uh . . . Mr. Frack, just out of curiosity, who was X. R. Parker?"

Frack smiles for the first time. "He's the author of your history book."

Very tricky.

I hate teachers who love to trick kids on tests. I feel my lip curl.

Derek catches my eye. We both frown, and then he whispers, "Watch this . . . give me a second."

Frack is now standing at his desk, his fist on the wood.

"Now, class, I have clerical work to do. So I'm going to pass out handouts. Read them and answer the questions on the bottom of the sheet."

Handouts. Again. That's the fourth time this week.

Just as I see Inky Grant taking out his baseball cards, and another kid start to draw dashes for a game of hangman, a round disc of light appears on Frack's cheek. A little quarter-sized reflection. The whole class is alert again. We watch the light as it slowly moves up Frack's red veiny nose. Then it moves to his eye.

There are a few very quiet giggles as Frack covers his brow with a hand, and looks toward the window.

But it isn't coming from there.

It's coming from Derek. Under his desk, Derek is flicking his wristwatch. The face of the watch is catching the sun and sending the round reflection to Frack's nose again.

Now there are more very muffled giggles.

Frack squints, which makes him look ridiculous.

I can't help myself. I laugh loudly, my honking, inhaling, goose laugh.

A mistake.

Frack pivots his tall skinny frame to look for where the laugh is coming from. I clamp my teeth and slurp in some air. He stares at me suspiciously, then walks to the wardrobe.

Derek grins at me again, then scribbles something on a sheet of loose-leaf paper.

As the latest handout reaches my desk, Derek passes the folded note to Inky, who stretches, as though to yawn, and drops it on the handout in front of me. It's a poem.

*2:15*
*Roses are red, violets are deep.*
*I'm failing history cause*
*Frack is a creep.*

I can't help it. I burst out honking.

This time, Frack's eyes immediately meet mine. And he begins walking toward me.

I quickly scrunch the note and drop it down my blouse just as Frack reaches my desk.

"And what was so funny, Missy?"

"Nothing, Mr. Frack."

"Really? Something was funny."

"No. Uh . . . no . . . I had an itch in my throat . . ."

"I see. And what's your name?"

"Uh . . . Molly . . . Sny . . . Snyder."

Everyone has turned in their seats to watch.

I hate being the focus of attention. Especially this kind of attention.

Frack is still standing over me, his fingers tapping my desk. "Well, Miss Snyder, why don't you tell the class the answers to the quiz. What was the date of the Boston Tea Party?"

He is so close I can smell him. My heart is pounding.

"Yes?"

"Um . . . I forget."

"You forget . . . or you don't know?"

"I don't know."

"I see. Then, what was the name of the ship?"

"Uh . . . I'm not sure . . ."

"You're not sure? Or you don't know?"

"I . . . I don't know." I can't help myself. I add, "I'm sure I don't know."

This guy makes a good kid bad.

Frack scowls at me. "Then how about this one, Missy. Who was responsible for that reflection in my eye?"

I scratch the desk with my fingernail.

"I want an answer. Monday detention unless I get an answer."

Monday. That's the newspaper tryouts.

My eyes meet his. I wish there was a fire. Or his heart would stop. Or there was an earthquake. Why can't a disaster happen when you need one.

"Mr. Frack, I . . . I don't know that either . . ." Smiling sincerely, I add, "I'm sure I don't know."

Just then there's a long loud clang. Then two more.

A nuclear alert. Or a nuclear alert drill.

Either way—thank you, God.

Frack stares at me for one quick second, then turns to the rest of the class and barks, "All right. Line up in front of the class. No running. No talking. No shoving."

And as he walks to the door, and I head for the line, I hold my breath.

Officially, he didn't give me detention.

Derek gets in line right behind me and whispers an apology.

I just nod with the dignity and nobility of a non-squealer.

Keeping my head down, I approach the door. If I don't make eye contact with Frack, he can't give me that detention.

I walk through the doorway, and file out into the hall where mobs of kids are already sitting against the walls.

I sit next to Laura.

She smiles at me and whispers, "And on top of everything . . . he has no lips . . ."

I honk. I double honk.

And in a second, I hear an icy voice. "Ah yes. Ms. Snyder . . ."

I look up.

"Monday detention." He smiles. "And don't forget it. Because—I'll be waiting for you."

# Chapter 5

Sitting on a bench along Verona Bay, I put down my backpack and try to forget about Frack.

I call Kathy but she's not home yet. So I'll hang around here for a while.

I open my notebook and write down the newspaper ideas I've thought of during the day.

I'd like to do an exposé on the girls' bathrooms because half of them don't work.

I'd call it "Shame of Our Stalls."

Or, I could do a piece on the Bryan swim team. They've come in last for the last ten years because they won't pay a coach enough money.

I'd call it "Shame of Our Crawls."

I love newspaper writing.

But I'm not going to get to do any if I don't get out of Frack's detention so I can go to the meeting.

Even if I go to the meeting, I still might not

make the paper. There are so many other kids trying out.

I can't believe I got off to such a bad start in
Frack's class. He's so unfair. I hate that.

Looking up from my book, I spot a little boy
pedaling past me on a bike. On Verona Bay, the sun
hits the water and forms a little green highway of
light across it. Fishermen are leaning against the
railing. Ice cream trucks are parked at the curb.

Verona is so beautiful in the fall. It makes me
feel better.

When you're in class, school seems like the most
important thing in the world.

But when you're outside, when you realize
you're just a little speck in the big universe, it sure
doesn't seem as important.

Getting up, I head for Kathy's again.

I turn down Dover Street, and half run to the
Marantz house. Knocking on the wooden door-
frame, I peek inside. No sound of Princess. No
sound at all.

"Kathy?" I call. "Are you there?"

There's no answer, but I think I hear music
coming from her bedroom.

I walk up the stairs to the dark rose door of her
room and rap against the huge blow-up of The
Grateful Dead.

Kathy is a total '60s music freak.

There is still no answer so I put my ear against
the door. All I hear is the Stones' "You Can't Always Get What You Want."

41

Then I do a stupid thing. I open the door.

Kathy and Nick are making out on her bed.

I'm backing right out when she spots me.

"Hi!" she says, untangling herself and sitting up.

"Ooh . . . sorry," I whisper hoarsely. "'Scuse me. Wrong house."

I slam the door behind me and lean my back against it while I slowly turn beet red.

In five seconds, Kathy is pushing the door against me.

As I move away, she eases out of her room to stand beside me. "Hii! I was just going to call you. Today isn't such a good day to go to the mall for me."

No kidding.

"That's Nick," she goes on. "I'm really sorry. I totally forgot. Totally. Until it was too late. I'm really sorry."

I can't look at her because I'm so mad.

She shrugs. "Nick's really cute though . . . isn't he?"

"He's okay."

"We were just . . . you know . . . kissing."

I play with the light switch next to my shoulder and shake my head. "I guess that's what they call 'heavy kissing,'" I say.

She grins, leans closer to me and whispers. "This is the first time I've ever . . . done anything. Please, don't be angry. I couldn't say no. And I think I'm in love. Are you angry?"

I shrug. "Well, I guess I understand. Maybe

42

when I fall in love, I'll be totally selfish and inconsiderate to my friends too."

"Good," she answers. "I'm glad you're not angry."

Her clothes are all messy and I can't help but stare as she tucks in her blouse. Her always frizzy hair is even wilder than usual, and the barrette that she wears at the nape of her neck is crooked.

"So," she says, readjusting it, "how've you been?"

"Great. Just absolutely great. Couldn't be better. So great . . ."

Just then, Nick peeks his head out of Kathy's door.

He looks like a football player. A big square face, a fat neck and a squat strong build. He has twinkly eyes and a nice grin though, so I suppose, feature for feature, he isn't bad looking.

"Hi, I'm Nick. You're . . ."

"Molly. Molly Snyder."

"Nice to meet you, Molly," he says.

"Likewise," I say.

The three of us stand there silently for a second.

"Look, Kath. I'm sorry I interrupted," I finally murmur. "I guess I'll go."

I want her to tell me to stay. I want her to make him go.

After all, how much necking can you do?

But all she says is, "I'll walk you to the door."

"Swell."

When we get to the porch, I look back at the

43

open curtains of the Marantzes' living room. Nick is standing there, staring.

"I hope you know what you're doing, Kath," I whisper.

"I don't. But if I had to wait 'til I knew what I was doing, I'd never get to do it. We have to break out sometime."

"Yeah." I point to my chin. "The only breaking out I'm doing is here. Occasionally, on my forehead." I grin at her, then unconsciously, because I feel more relaxed, I sit down on the stoop.

She doesn't.

I stand up. "Well," I say. "I can't really stay . . ."

"Yeah. But I'll call you."

"Will you?"

"I will. I will." She turns around to look at Nick. "What do you think of him?"

I look again. "He looks . . . like the President of St. Bart's," I say.

Wow. What a subtle insult.

"Thanks," she says. She doesn't even get it—that's how good an insult it was.

Now I smile. "Well, see ya around." And, walking back down the street, I can feel Kathy's eyes following me, but I don't look back.

She calls after me. I pretend not to hear.

Then I hear the sound of feet and feel a tap on my shoulder.

"Listen, I'm going to my dad's for the weekend, but how about going to the movies Sunday night. What do you say?"

I make myself not smile. I tense up the part of myself that's softening.

"That's a possibility."

"There's this new movie at the Oceana. *Love in the Fiords,* about this Hispanic boy and this Jewish girl and their parents drive them apart and he starts taking drugs and gets into a car accident and loses his sight, but they run away together to get him an operation in Scandinavia . . ."

Even though that sounds slightly tempting, I say no. "My dad read this new book about teenagers and now he wants us to spend every Sunday evening together for 'family time' or 'quality time' or something psychological like that."

"Oh. You wouldn't lie to get out of it, would you?"

I shake my head and she nods like I'm hopeless.

"Okay, then, I know what." She hesitates. "Let's walk to school Monday. I'll pick you up. All right?"

I nod. Not only am I melting, but I feel a little bad for the Nick putdown, even though Kathy didn't catch it.

I look back at Nick. "Fine. That would be good, but are you sure he won't mind?"

"I'll explain."

"He's adorable . . . actually."

Which makes her smile. "Thanks. So, see you first thing Monday. And, I . . . miss you."

"I miss you too."

We walk a little more, and now I tell her what

45

happened in Frack's class. When I ask her advice, she gives me an outrageous suggestion.

"Kathy! Me? I couldn't . . ."

She grins. "Sure you could."

"Gee, I've only been in school a week. It's not my style."

"Molly, it's the only logical answer. Remember my philosophy, 'Life is short. And then you die.' Besides, it would be good for you."

I nod. "Well, maybe. I'll think about it."

At the corner, we say good-bye and she dashes back to her house. I walk a little farther and then half turn to see her reach the Marantz porch and embrace Nick. As they kiss, his hands move up and down her back.

Yuk.

Not yuk that what she's doing is bad.

Yuk to what I'm feeling.

Which is jealous as hell.

# Chapter 6

It's just my dad, Billy and me at the table for Friday night dinner because my mom's cold has gotten worse and she's gone to bed.

So I've whipped up a tuna casserole and some frozen green beans.

I even used the homemade noodles my mom made last weekend, so it's pretty good.

Luckily, so far no one has asked me about my life because the big news of the day is that Billy has already gotten caught cutting classes.

My dad is so mad that the three of us are sitting at the table in total silence.

The only sounds are forks hitting teeth.

My dad is extra angry because not only did Billy cut, he told the attendance office that my mother couldn't come in for a meeting because she was permanently attached to a dialysis machine.

It's so quiet I can hear Billy's Sprite going down his throat.

Finally, my dad turns to me to take his mind off his firstborn.

"So, how was school, Molly?"

"It's okay."

"Good. Starting new places is always tough."

"I know, Dad."

"But it always seems worse than it is."

"Yes, Dad."

"The more you put into something, the more you'll get out of it."

"That's probably true, Dad."

I love my father very much. He's a great lawyer. He's kind and generous and smart.

Unfortunately, he also talks like a Hallmark card.

He swallows a bite of tunafish and continues. "How's Latin? Can you say anything yet?"

"Uh . . . *amo, amas, amat.*"

He beams. "You're so smart. And how's history? My favorite subject . . ."

"How about more noodles, Dad?" I plop some more food on my dad's plate, and then on Billy's.

"Well, just remember, if you study a little bit every day you won't fall behind."

"I'll remember, Dad."

Billy looks up at me. "Molly, you're nearest the refrigerator. Get some more soda, okay?"

That was a dumb move. My dad glares over at him. "Billy, Molly is not your maid. She's done enough, as usual. Get it yourself."

"Okay, okay." He gets up, and brings another bottle of Sprite to the table.

We continue to eat in silence.

I wish my mom was feeling better. She'd lighten the mood.

Finally, when my brother starts tapping on the table with his fingertips, my father explodes. "You know, I can't believe the year is starting this way, young man!"

"Dad, I said I was sorry. I cut one class. Geez, I'm sorry."

"You're always sorry, Billy. High school counts. Why do I get the feeling that Mom and I are going to show up at Bryan more than you will again!"

I can't help it. I laugh.

"It's not like you don't have the ability, either," my dad shouts. "You have a high IQ. It is such a waste. . ."

I usually like to see Billy fry a little, but it's so uncomfortable that I decide to try to lighten things up myself.

"Hey, Dad, you can't believe how bad my history teacher is. He's boring. And he gives unbelievably long homeworks. And he actually looks like a rat. His face is gray and he has this pointy nose . . ."

My brother looks up. "You have Frack the Hack, don't you?"

I nod.

"Jim Widener, who's on the track team with me, says he's certifiably insane. He gives detentions like crazy. Mike missed so many practices, he almost didn't make the team. You're doomed."

My dad shakes his head. "Billy, don't poison

49

your sister's mind against a teacher. Molly, be patient. You're such a good student. When he gets to know you, he'll love you."

I think of my detention. Frack will have plenty of time to get to know me. But I just say, "I'll try, Dad."

My father nods. "Good. That's all you can do. There are all kinds of people in this world and you have to learn to get along with them."

"Right." I pick up my empty plate. "I don't know what we have for dessert."

A soft holler comes from the bedroom.

It's my mom. "There's homemade apple crisp in the freezer. You just have to microwave it."

My dad and I look at each other and grin.

He calls back into the bedroom. "How about a stuffed mom doll, dear? You wind it up and it says, 'You just have to microwave it'?"

"Very funny, dear," she calls back. "Although . . . that's not a bad idea. You might have something there." Her voice sounds far away, as though it's coming from underwater, but it still has a smile in it. In five minutes, she's walking out of her bedroom in her pink bathrobe.

"Talking mom doll. I like it." She grins.

She looks pale, but she doesn't look like she has a cold. Maybe she's just worried about her job.

So I venture helpfully. "You could also have a talking brother doll," I say. "You wind it up and it stays home from school." I honk at my own joke.

Billy makes a face at me. "And a talking sister doll. You wind it up and it's flat chested."

I kick him under the table.

"Children, children!" my mother says.

My father looks at her and puts his hand gently on her arm.

"How're you feeling, dear?"

She looks at him and sighs.

My dad gets up and puts his arm around her and kisses her temple. She smiles and shows her dimples.

My mom has even bigger dimples than my brother.

In her high school yearbook, they wrote under her picture, "With her dimples and sweetness, she will conquer the world."

My dad squeezes her hand again, and she nuzzles his neck.

After all these years, my parents still act very lovey-dovey.

It's kind of nice except when they do it in public.

"Most of our worries never happen," my father whispers in my mom's ear. She nods, then turns to me, smiling again as cheerfully as possible. "What were you all saying about that history teacher?"

"He stinks." I look at my dad. "But when he gets to know me, he'll love me."

Tightening the belt on her robe, she sits down at the table and begins to eat off my plate.

"Tell me."

"All I know is if you wound up a Frack doll, it'd say, 'Detention for breathing, Missy.'"

51

When my dad and Billy are looking away, she mouths the words, "Did *you* get detention?"

My mom doesn't miss a trick.

I nod, clench my teeth and widen my eyes to indicate I don't want anyone else to know.

She clears her throat and says, "Uh . . . Moll . . . you want to walk me to the bedroom? I have some great earrings I want to show you."

At her bedroom door she says, "Listen, honey, I know that's upsetting. But it's no big deal. Trust me, you're going to be happy at Bryan. I'm never wrong . . . when I'm right."

I nod and she kisses me on the forehead. "I think I'll lie down now. But if you're really worried, tell Dad. He'll understand."

"He'll lecture me."

She squeezes my hand. "Try. . ."

Back at the table, my dad studies me too.

"Anything going on I should know about?" he asks lightly.

I confess.

My dad looks surprised, then upset, then sympathetic. "Hey, everybody gets a detention once. I'm sure it wasn't your fault." Puckering his lips, he makes a kissing noise. "Don't be so upset . . . really."

Billy shakes his head. "Typical. I get detention and you're ready to send me to reform school. She gets detention and you throw her a kiss!"

My father glares at Billy. "That's because, young man, you're proud of it. This is her first. You have your own chair in the detention room."

I swallow a laugh. Just barely.

Billy glares at me again, mutters something and spears a solid chunk of tuna casserole with his fork. Just as I'm standing to pick up the plates, I feel a smack against my cheek. A piece of fish has been flicked at my neck.

"Billy!" I blurt.

"Young man, that's enough! Leave the table!"

"Fine with me!" Billy shouts, and shoves his chair back too. "That's just fine with me!"

And then there is the familiar sound of Billy storming into his room and the door slamming behind him.

Then there is the familiar sight of my father shaking his head.

He looks at me, frustration on his face, and then puts his hand lovingly over mine with one of his "Thank goodness one of my children is sweet and responsible" looks. And while I try to smile at him maturely, I think of Frack again. And my newspaper tryout.

It would be immature and irresponsible to cut detention.

Kathy's advice was right.

I think I'll play hooky.

# Chapter 7

Click.

It's 2:30 Monday afternoon and I'm lying on the sofa with the remote control in my hand.

I can definitely get into this.

Except for having to cancel out on walking to school with Kathy, hooky was a brilliant idea.

I love being in the house by myself. It's so . . . so . . . serene.

I haven't moved from a prone position in five hours, except to hunt for food.

I've watched three soap operas, four quiz shows and a talk show about transvestites who want to raise children.

There was even a program on educational tv about Denmark during World War II. I never would have learned that much if I'd gone to school.

But now I have to get up and go over to Bryan.

That's the only bad thing about hooky. It's hard

to muster up the energy to get back into the world. Even to go to a *Bugle* meeting.

But I get up, stretch and head for the closet.

Putting on the new English Fog raincoat my mom bought me to look like a reporter, I scan the room for evidence.

The afghan on the couch. I refold it neatly.

Popcorn on the floor. I get down on my hands and knees and pick the kernels up from the rug, including one I'd crushed into microscopic pieces.

Because of my brother, my parents tend to frown on hooky. They don't realize every once in a while it's a necessity. Neither did I, until now.

I give the house a final inspection, and then walk out the door.

Instead of heading for Bryan along the bay, I detour down some side streets.

No one would be suspicious if I walked along the bay at three o'clock, but playing hooky puts you in a sneaky mood.

At the main entrance, I even avoid the front doors. Ducking in the back, I tiptoe up the stairs and head for the fourth floor, keeping an eye out for Frack.

My heart is pounding nervously by the time I get to room 402. Stenciled on the door are the words: NEWSPAPER OFFICE. An oak tag sign says WELCOME.

As I sidle into a backseat and look around, I take a deep breath and relax.

I can't help feeling the thrill of deceit. Now I

55

understand why Billy, no matter how much he gets yelled at, is so cheerful all the time.

A curly headed boy, in a three-piece suit, wearing thick glasses, is in the middle of his speech. On the blackboard behind him, he's written his name: Jeremy Backman, Editor-in-Chief.

He holds up a plaque. "And our final award came last year for Serena Newell's perspicacious feature story about the lonely swan of Verona Bay. I called it 'Swan of these Days.'" He smiles wisely, his thumbs hanging from his vest pockets.

Jeremy looks and sounds forty years old.

My eyes scan the room. Derek is two rows ahead of me, Michael two seats away from him. Karen Aaron, Frack's pet, is on one side of Derek, the other seat is empty.

Just as I'm about to move into it, Laura does. But then she sees me, pats the empty seat next to her, and I take it.

I'm sitting behind a boy who's wider than the Great Wall of China, but I'm glad I'm there.

"Did you cut today?" Karen leans over Laura and whispers to me.

I nod.

"Really? Well, I think you ought to know that Frack asked about you. I think he was suspicious."

"He did? He was?"

My stomach sinks.

Laura nudges me. "Don't worry, Molly. Just bring a note."

Good idea. I smile at her.

Laura's so delicate looking in her flower print dress. Her voice is so quiet and friendly.

"What did I miss in class?" I whisper.

She shakes her head. "Nothing. Handout number five. And a speech about how children in the colonies weren't spoiled like kids today."

I grin. "Fascinating. So sorry I missed it."

Laura chuckles. Derek looks over and says "Hi." So does Michael.

Nice.

Jeremy clears his throat. "All right," he says. "I know there was a rumor that you should bring your own assignments. Well, not for our first trial. Since you don't know Bryan High well yet, we don't believe that would be efficacious."

I squint at Laura. Perspicacious. Efficacious. Jeremy sounds like the host of "Masterpiece Theatre."

She whispers to me, "He's studying for his SAT's. I know. My brother Todd and he take the same tutoring class. They're studying 'ous' words."

Jeremy clears his throat. "Ms. Medina apologizes for not being here, by the way. Her third grader is the starring duck in a school play." He picks up a sheet of assignments from a messy pile on the desk before him. "Now, I think it would be auspicious to begin . . ."

Sixty people move in their seats, or shift the papers on their desks or nod.

"All right, first let's do some basic news stories. We need a piece on the new telescope on the roof."

57

A boy in front gets the job.

"A piece on the science research awards . . ."

Lots of hands come into view. Mine goes up too, but Jeremy can't see me and doesn't call on me.

It goes like that for a while. Assignment after assignment, and I'm not picked.

Laura gets chosen to interview the girls' track coach.

Michael gets a piece on Mr. Rubin, the school janitor who's been running a clothing drive for poor kids. Great assignment.

Karen Aaron volunteers to write an editorial on fall foliage. Yuk.

I wish I had longer arms.

Maybe I could sit on The Wall's shoulders.

Jeremy looks down the sheet of paper on which the assignments have been written, frowns and then puts it down.

"Uh . . . we have a rather multitudinous turnout today. And I have to admit that uh . . . it's hard to come up with sixty plum assignments. But every assignment can be a challenge." He smiles reassuringly. "So, I did make up a second list." Picking up another sheet of paper, he reads.

"Ms. Abigail Brewer. Who'd like to do a story about her? The Assistant School Nurse."

No one raises a hand. Nurse Brewer came into our homeroom on Friday. She's six foot three, wheezes and has a mustache.

"Really, this could be an interesting piece. The personal anguish of a woman who has to deal with lice day in and day out hasn't been explored." Silence.

A girl to my left reluctantly raises her hand.

The choices are thinning out.

Jeremy looks down at his sheet again. "We do have a new team forming—duplicate bridge. None of the upperclass reporters jumped at it. Perhaps because only one kid is on the team so far. Any interest?"

Three kids volunteer, including me. I'm desperate.

But still, I'm not picked.

And, after two more unbelievably boring assignments that I can't even make myself volunteer for, Jeremy puts down the second sheet.

"Okay," he says. "Has anyone not been given an assignment?"

My hand goes up to half-mast. So does my body as I finally force myself to half rise in my chair. "Uh . . ." I say, "I haven't."

Jeremy meets my eyes, frowns, then looks back at his sheet.

My voice wants to blurt out, "Maybe I could suggest an assignment," but my lips won't move. I feel so shy.

"Well, um . . . let's see." He picks up a torn piece of paper. "Wait a sec—I have something here. Josh Newell, a senior, had to cancel out. That leaves his assignment uh . . . unassigned. Let me see what it was. . ."

He studies the sheet, then looks up thoughtfully.

59

Is it my imagination or has the blood left his face?

"Um . . . this piece is important. We'd need it for the next issue. It's not easy. It'll take a good reporter. It's a challenge. . . Can you handle a challenge?"

I nod enthusiastically. "Uh huh!"

But Jeremy frowns. "On the other hand, maybe I should do this one . . ."

I shake my head eagerly, forgetting my shyness. "Jeremy, I can do it! What is it?"

He bites his lip and shakes his head. "It's . . . uh . . . it's to interview the freshman history teacher, Mr. Henry Frack."

I slump back in my chair.

"You know him?"

I get back up on my knees. "Uh huh."

"He's celebrating his thirtieth anniversary of teaching at Bryan. We have to do this story."

Jeremy looks at me sympathetically as I try to think through a haze of confusion. "Let me think," he says. "Let me think . . . wait. I have another idea!"

"Good!"

"Yeah. Would you be interested in doing a piece about the vegetable garden? This is the first year the asparagus will come up. . ."

I shake my head.

"You can take your choice."

Great. I have a choice between a flower pot and a crackpot.

I think for a minute.

I want to make the paper. Frack is a tough assignment but they need the article. They need it bad.

There's so much competition. This could be a real opportunity.

If things are going to get better at Bryan, I've got to be optimistic again. Happy again. Hopeful again.

Like, maybe Frack would be flattered to be interviewed.

Maybe we'll talk and he'll pour his heart out to me.

Although, I hope it doesn't land on my foot. It's probably made of cement.

"What do you say?" Jeremy asks.

"I'll do it!" I answer.

"Really?"

"I'm not sure . . ."

Jeremy grins. "You better talk to me after the meeting."

# Chapter 8

I wait patiently as Jeremy talks to a few other kids. When they finally leave, he looks me over. "What's your name, anyway?"

"Molly. Molly Snyder."

"Not the Molly Snyder who was editor of the Whitman *Wire*?"

"Right." I turn up the Velcro collar of my English Fog raincoat to make me seem more like a reporter. Immediately, the Velcro sticks to my neck. "How'd you know?"

"My brother Colin was in your year at Whitman. He used to bring home the paper. It was good. I always admired your writing. It was very . . . unpretentious."

"Thanks. That's very . . . solicitous . . . felicitous . . . nice of you to say."

"So, what do you want to do?"

I shake my head. "I don't know."

"Well, if you don't want to, I understand."

"Yeah. I don't. And then again, I do. I do and I don't. Definitely."

He holds his chin with two fingers. "I'll tell you this, Molly. Maybe Frack will be tough, but if you can get a story, you really will be in like Flynn on the *Bugle*."

"Really?"

"Definitely." He lowers his voice and speaks confidentially. "You know, I can only accept nine new reporters and we have sixty kids, twenty of whom were editors of their junior high papers. The best articles will be published, and those are the kids who will make the *Bugle*. And I'm telling you, this is an article we *want*. You follow my drift?"

My eyes drift up and down as I nod.

"Good. Frack's a challenge, sure. It'll take boldness. Initiative. It would be great if you could get behind the man, behind the image. You have a lot of potential. You could be an important writer here."

"Really?"

When someone tells me I have potential, I'll do anything.

"So, what do you say? You want to dig deep inside yourself and go that extra mile?"

My heart pounds. "Okay! Sure!"

"Great!" He puts his arm around me and escorts me to the door. "And you know what I want most of all. I want you to have fun with it!"

I hobble along next to him because the bottom Velcro snap is sticking to my tights. "Fun with it . . . right!"

He opens the door. "Which won't be easy because I doubt if he'll even talk to you, but hey, good luck!"

And in a second, I'm out in the hall, alone.

But as I walk toward the exit, I decide again not to worry. My heart fills with the promise of my soon to be fulfilled potential.

"Mr. Frack," I mutter to myself as I hobble down the stairs, holding the edge of my raincoat. "I'm Molly Snyder, and I'd like to talk to you about a little piece we're doing about your career here—your miserable, loathsome career."

And I giggle all the way to Home Acres.

At home, I make a pee stop and then head for the backyard where Billy is shooting baskets.

I have to ask him an important favor before my parents get back from work.

He misses a shot.

"Nice try," I say enthusiastically.

He takes another shot and misses again.

"Almost!" I say even more enthusiastically.

He gives me a suspicious look.

I better get to it.

"Billy, I need a favor. A tiny tiny tiny favor and I need it before Mom and Dad get back."

"They already got back." He walks to the edge of the driveway and shoots from the side. "They went out again."

"How come?" I put out my hands for the ball. I like basketball too.

"I don't know." He shoots. "And the basket is

64

in!" He looks at me, dribbles, then shoots again. "It was a little weird." He retrieves the ball.

"What do you mean?" I ask, sticking my hands out again.

He ignores them again and bounces the ball noisily against a metal garbage can. "I don't know. Mom came rushing into the house and she seemed upset. And then Dad followed her into the bedroom. And then when they came out, he said he was taking her out for dinner."

"Hmmm." My stomach tightens. "Fight?"

"Mom and Dad? Nah." He looks at me. "I heard something about the doctor . . . she had another checkup for her flu or something . . . I don't know."

"Hmmm." I sit down right on the driveway. "I wonder what's going on? You sure it wasn't a fight."

Even though my parents seem very happily married, you can never tell.

Billy sits down next to me with a thud. He's all sweaty and stinky. I move over just a tad.

"So, what do you want and how much are you willing to pay?" he asks.

"Well," I swallow. "I . . . uh . . . I played hooky today."

His eyes widen. "You? Why?"

"To get out of detention, of course."

I wish it weren't so dark out so I could see his face.

He pinches my arm. "What's going on? Is this

65

*Invasion of the Body Snatchers?* This can't be Ms. Sweet and Perfect."

"I'm not perfect! I'm not sweet!"

"You're telling me."

I take the ball from him nervously and tell him the whole story. "So, I . . . I need an absent note. I don't want to have to ask Frack for this interview at the same time he's giving me another detention."

"Makes sense."

I shoot the ball from a sitting position. It hits the garage.

"Anyway, I thought to myself, who could help me? Who is practically an artist at absent notes. Who do I respect in this field. . ."

"Five bucks."

"Three . . ."

"Five. Take it or leave it."

"I'll take it." And we head for the house.

While I put the frozen tv dinners in the microwave, Billy sits at the table.

"So," he begins, "what kind of excuse do you want? Sore throat, flu, unexplained exhaustion . . ."

I take out some plates and forks and plunk them in front of him. I throw a napkin on his plate.

"What do you suggest?" I say respectfully.

He scratches his nose. "Well, I think it's best to work with something you can use again. A mysterious low-grade fever is always good."

I bring out glasses. "I don't know about a low-grade fever. Frack is very distrustful. We need something better."

"Right." Billy raps his plate with a fork. "Let me think . . . You wouldn't want some sort of bladder condition?"

Locked bathrooms. Dialysis. Bladder conditions. My brother is definitely into kidneys.

"Absolutely not."

He shrugs. "Okay. Okay. It's just that kidney problems always sound real. Although, if you want the best, the top of the line, how about colitis?"

I wrinkle my nose. "I'll settle for less."

He seems disappointed, but says, grudgingly, "Well, I guess we can always go with the old standby, a minor sore throat."

"I'll take it." Just saying it, my throat starts to hurt.

As I bring the chicken dinners to the table, he prints the note.

"You understand, of course," he says in a serious tone, "that you can write the actual note like a kid. It's the signature they look at."

"Right."

His arms stretch out before him and he makes circles with his neck. "You need to relax first." He wiggles his fingers, and breathes deeply a few times through his nose.

Then he picks up a pen. "I think I'm ready."

"Need anything to drink?" I whisper, mesmerized.

"No. No drinking." He takes out a folded piece

67

of paper from a notebook, and flattens it with the heel of his hand. "This is a photocopy of Dad's signature. He has a great signature, so it takes a while."

I pat him on the back. "Hey, take your time."

I stare as he contemplates my father's name. Then he looks up at me. He pats the table. "Sit down. If you're into hooky and detention, I think this is a skill you ought to learn."

"Hmmm . . . yeah. Okay." When I sit, he hands me a pen and some blank sheets of paper. "Thanks."

"Now, look at Dad's name. It's the *S* that's tough. Very fancy. And the final *t*. Big flourish. Study it."

I look at my dad's signature and then start to write.

"Hold it! Hold it!" says Billy. "This takes a while. This is a process. Slow down and we'll do it right."

He sounds just like my father.

"Doing it quickly, but wrong, takes longer than doing it right," I say, mimicking another of my dad's lines.

We both laugh.

Billy does have great dimples, for a brother.

"Come on now. Let's get serious, Molly."

And we begin to work.

We study, we stare, and then we trace my dad's signature in the air above his name.

Finally, we begin to write, moving the pens on our blank sheets as our eyes follow the lines of my dad's name.

68

Billy's looks good.

*Mr. Stuart Snyder*

Mine doesn't.

*Mr. Stuart Snyder*

"I stink at this," I say.

He leans over my paper and scrunches his chin up in thought. "Huh . . . maybe I'm not explaining it right. Tell you what. Try one letter at a time. If you can get that, then you can move on to the next. Don't be discouraged."

I smile at him thankfully and try again.

I try ten, twenty, thirty times.

By the fortieth time, it isn't bad. It looks like an *S* my dad might have written when he was thirteen.

I keep going.

"This isn't easy, Billy."

"Nothing worthwhile is easy, young lady!"

We giggle again.

After twenty minutes, I manage a few full *Stuart Snyders*. Billy studies my latest attempt.

"Better. Much better." He looks closely, moving his finger along the signature, stopping at the final squiggle at the end of *Snyder*. "Yeah. Quite good."

"Really?" I say, drinking in the praise.

He stares at my forgery with admiration. "Definitely. I'm telling you, this signature is A+ work."

"Billy, you're . . . you're . . ." I want to say he's

69

wonderful but I don't want to go too far. "Thanks . . . And I mean it."

"Forget it." And he puts out his hand. I give him five.

"Hey, doofus," he says. "I didn't want a high five. I want a green five." Luckily, he smiles.

I reach into my wallet for the money, and give it to him.

Five whole bucks.

I hope this works.

# Chapter 9

Billy pours a carload of Cap'n Crunch and then slices little chunks of banana that fall off his knife and into his bowl.

We're sitting at the breakfast table.

I'm wearing my new blue tank top. It's a little tight. A little daring.

My dad is reading the paper, as usual, and my mom is in the bathroom. Every once in a while, my dad's nose appears. He glances at us and then looks for my mom.

I've tried to study them both but I can't tell what's going on.

I hate when my parents have secrets.

Why do parents think they're protecting kids when they walk around with a face that says "I'm worried about something," but a mouth that says "Wrong? Nothing's wrong." I worry anyway, only I don't know what to worry about so I worry about everything.

Billy pours half a carton of milk into his bowl.

In two minutes, he's finished his cereal and is reaching for a donut.

I'm too nervous to eat. Asking Frack for an interview. Getting the note past him. This is a big day.

My dad looks up at me. "Isn't that shirt a little . . . snug?"

I swallow. "You think so?" And when he nods, I run into my room, put on a turtleneck and run back out. Maybe tomorrow I'll stretch the tank top a little and wear it. I want to. A lot.

Just as I sit down, the phone rings.

It's Kathy. "Molly!" she says warmly. "How was hooky?"

I whisper into the phone. "Excellent. It was very . . . educational."

She giggles. "Listen, I forgot. I can't walk with you this morning. I have my first student council meeting before first period. Nick is picking me up."

"Damn."

"I know. We have to stop *not* meeting like this. But I'll call you later."

"Okay."

"I don't even know anybody. I just know they'll all be rich or their parents will be famous. And nobody will talk to me and . . ."

"Sure they will. You're with Nick. Don't worry."

What I want to say is, "Why the hell do you want to be with those people," but I don't. I just say we'll talk later and then hang up. As I do, my mother comes out of the bathroom, still in her bathrobe, and sits at the table. My dad pours her some coffee.

Donut sugar falls on my hands. It's Billy, getting up to go.

"So, see you later." He turns to my mom. "Oh, by the way," he asks super casually. "How was the doctor? Did you go back to him for new pills or something?"

She looks up. "No. Not exactly."

My father puts down his paper.

Their eyes meet.

"Kids. Billy, Molly," my mother begins. "I don't want you to worry."

I immediately begin to worry.

"What's the matter?" Billy asks.

My mother sighs. My father says, "It seems like your mother has a little walking pneumonia."

My mom doesn't say anything.

My dad smiles. "It's not serious though. It's more like limping pneumonia."

That makes me smile but my mom frowns. She looks uncomfortable.

"They want me to go into the hospital, just for a few days. It might be less. But I have to go."

"That doesn't sound so serious," I say.

On the other hand, she doesn't look sick. I don't get it.

"Mom will be at Verona Hospital," Dad continues. "There's no need to visit today. But maybe tomorrow . . ."

"You can call me after school." As Billy gives her a kiss good-bye, my mom smiles, but it's not one of her best.

"Okay," Billy calls as he reaches the door. "I'll call after track."

"Be good." she says to him.

"Of course." And he's gone.

While my mother sips her coffee, I stare into her brain. But I can't see anything.

She catches me. "Molly, everything's fine. I know you're a worrier, but I'm sure everything's fine."

As I give my dad a kiss good-bye, he adds, "Absolutely. Now get going. The early bird, and all that."

"Right."

I give my mother a big hug and then, I'm out of there.

At 1:59, the last period warning bell rings. Walking down the hall to history, I suddenly lose my nerve.

My hand reaches for the backdoor knob of room 345. It's 2:01, class has started, but my wrist won't turn.

I'm reciting one of my father's most useless sayings, "The worst thing we have to fear is fear itself," when suddenly a hand clutches my shoulder.

I jump three feet.

"Billy!"

He's wearing his gray sweat pants and blue and white Bryan shirt.

"I'm on my way to track. Just thought I'd check on you," he says.

My hand regrips the doorknob. "I'm just going in. See you later."

He doesn't move.

"So, see ya," I repeat. "It's a shame to waste such a great absent note on just one day's absence. Maybe I should stay home longer. Like a month."

Billy snorts softly. "Molly, you can do this. I don't know about your *Bugle* thing, but the note's top quality. It'll be fine. I worked hard. Now, open the door!"

"Billy . . ."

"Moll, you have to. C'mon."

"I can't."

"You can."

"I can't."

"Then let me put it another way." He takes my wrist with one hand, opens the door with the other hand and shoves me into room 345. I land right on top of Michael's desk.

"Hi," Michael murmurs in surprise. "Feel free to drop in anytime."

"Hi," I say, forgetting all about Frack. "Sorry."

As I get off his desk, the entire class is looking at me.

I turn to the front of the room. "Hello, Mr. Frack," I say, sweeter than sugar. "I'm sorry I'm late. I was discussing irrational numbers with Mrs. Bloom. I'm really sorry."

Mr. Frack runs his hand along his shiny head and scowls.

"Just get to a seat, young lady! And where were

you yesterday?" He walks toward me as my knees lock in place.

"I was . . . ill." I wave the note in front of him, then try to move toward a desk.

"May I look at that note, please."

I hand it over nervously.

He studies it, then looks at me, then studies it again, frowning.

"And how's your throat now, Missy?" he finally asks.

"It uh . . . still hurts a lot, but I didn't want to miss another day."

"I'll bet. You can make up detention today. And you're lucky. I won't be there."

"Yes, Mr. Frack."

He returns my creative writing, along with another piece of paper. "This is sheet number seven. Read it and answer the questions at the bottom of the page."

"Yes, Mr. Frack. I will, Mr. Frack. Thank you, Mr. Frack."

"Now," he says to the rest of the class, "I have to leave for a few minutes. This class had better be quiet until I get back."

"Yes, Mr. Frack."

And he's gone.

Immediately, a low buzz breaks out. Kids start talking. Notes start being passed. Inky takes out a small pack of baseball cards and shows them to a kid on his right. Derek and Michael begin to play hangman from opposite sides of the room. After

Derek mouths a letter, Michael either nods or makes a cut sign against his throat.

Just as I'm trying to figure out Michael's seven letter word, I get a rap note that everybody's adding lines to. So far it reads:

> *I have a class late in the day*
> *Which never seems to go away.*
> *I groan, I yawn, I even scream*
> *But I just never get to dream. Danny L.*
> *If only I could go to sleep*
> *I'd dream of ways to get that bleep.*
> *He's old and frail and very boring*
> *But still he'd know if I was snoring.*
> *Laura S.*

I grin, think for a sec and then add my own.

> *This, I'm afraid, can no longer be*
> *Due to my average,*
> *Which is now thirty three. Molly S.*

Laura reads it, laughs and starts passing it around just as the door opens and Frack strides back in.

The room is hushed immediately. I keep my eye on the note. When it passes again, I grab it. I don't want to get into more trouble just before I'm about to ask Frack for that interview.

Heading for the front desk, Frack picks up the latest handout.

"So," he says, "who knows the answer to question number one."

Five kids raise their hands.

Naturally, he calls on a kid who's hand is down. Inky.

"Uh . . ." Inky stammers.

"Uh? Is 'uh' a word? I haven't noticed it in the dictionary lately." Frack smiles. The man only smiles when something's *not* funny. "I'm waiting . . ."

"I don't know ques . . . question number one," Inky stutters.

Frack narrows his gaze. "I'm not surprised. Perhaps because you were playing with whatever you're hiding beneath your desk instead of reading."

Inky says nothing, but I can hear his heart pounding as Frack starts toward him. Even the stains on Inky's fingers turn pale, and as the poor kid tries to slip the cards into his desk, Frack grabs them.

"I'll take those!"

In a second, he's unbanded the pack of cards and begun ripping them up, slowly.

Tears immediately come to Inky's eyes. "Sir . . . those were valuable . . . one of those was a rookie Dwight Goo . . ." Little teardrops plop onto Inky's cheeks.

You can feel the whole class hating Frack, but the man seems oblivious as he shakes his head.

"Tuesday detention for you, young man!" And he heads back to the front of the room.

Patting Inky on the back, I pretend not to see the tears on his cheeks and whisper, "I hope he falls into an open manhole."

"Ms. Snyder . . ."

My eyes look up, into Frack's eyes.

"Perhaps you can tell us the answer to the first question. Taxation without representation?"

Luckily, I know the answer from fourth grade.

"Taxation without representation means that the colonists were being forced to pay taxes even though they had no say in how they were governed."

I lean back and relax.

"And . . ."

And? He wants more. The man is never satisfied until you say something wrong.

Luckily, I realize that I know one more fact. But should I say it?

Frack frowns impatiently.

I say it. "Actually, it was not reasonable for a British colony to expect representation in those days. That's why some historians say that we just used the saying 'taxation without representation' as an excuse for the revolution we wanted anyway."

Frack nods, surprised. "That's correct. And where did you learn that?"

I try to fake it. "On a special program about American history."

"Really?" Now he is impressed. "Public television?"

"No. A beer commercial. It was on one of those Historical Moments."

The whole class bursts out laughing as I close my eyes.

I can't help it. The laughs are worth Frack's glare.

"I see." He turns stiffly to speak to the class. "Can you imagine how much she'd learn if she actually read a book instead of watching all that garbage?"

Can you imagine how much I'd learn if he actually taught me something?

But as Frack nods reluctantly to me and then moves on to the next victim, I breath a sigh of relief.

When the final bell rings and kids rush out to go home, I stand near the closets, and then approach the front desk.

Uh . . . sir . . ." I begin in a low voice.

He unwraps a mint, pops it into his mouth and continues to gather papers, ignoring me.

"Uh, Mr. Frack . . ." I raise my voice a little.

"Yes?" He looks up. "Are you in the first committee?"

Laura, Derek and Michael are standing in the corner, waving at me.

"Committee?" I ask as Frack holds up a folder and Laura comes over and gets it.

She whispers to me, "I forgot to tell you. He assigned committees yesterday."

Frack stares at me. "Yes. You were absent," he gestures to Laura's departing body, "so join theirs."

"Okay." Then, after a slow swallow, I begin again. "Uh, Mr. Frack?"

He looks up from the papers he's shuffling. "Now what?"

I clear my throat again. "Sir, I . . . uh . . . have

80

been . . . uh . . . privileged to be assigned to interview you for the Bryan *Bugle*."

Gathering the attendance sheet and a folder into his arms, he rises from his chair and walks toward the door.

I follow him. "Uh, Mr. Frack. Sir. Because it's your thirtieth anniversary, the *Bugle* has asked me . . ."

He turns around. "I heard you. I don't have time for interviews."

Out of the corner of my eye I spot Derek, Michael and Laura, trying to look like they're not eavesdropping, which they are.

"Mr. Frack, it won't take long. And you're my tryout assignment. I . . ."

He scowls. "You start doing *my* assignments. That's what you better worry about, young lady!"

"But Mr. Frack, if you don't agree to an interview, I won't make the *Bugle* . . ."

He smiles. "That's not *my* problem." And he shuffles away quickly and moves across the hall right to the Faculty Lounge. Pushing open the door, he disappears behind it before I can say another word.

"Damn!" I mutter.

Derek moves up beside me. "Not a nice guy."

Michael and Laura walk over as I exhale a clomp of air.

"What are you going to do, Molly?" Laura asks.

I shake my head. "I don't know. I just know that I hate that man. I loathe that man. I despise that man!"

I feel steam in my ears and my face getting hot. "I . . . I have a good mind to . . ."

Derek grimaces too. "To what? Paint his bald head red?"

I shake my head, and my teeth clamp so hard my jaw hurts.

"To what?" Laura asks.

"I . . . well . . . I don't know." My mind begins racing. "Maybe . . . maybe I'll do the article anyway. Without him. And . . . write the truth!"

Michael's eyes widen skeptically. "Why would you want to do that?"

I look at him, my jaw loosening a little. "Because . . . because I'm an investigative reporter. And nobody, not even Woodward and Bernstein, has ever written a piece about a bad teacher, a mean teacher."

"Wow!" Michael says, as Derek pulls me over to the side of the hall by my notebook, and Michael and Laura follow.

"That's some great idea," Laura says.

I nod. "Yeah."

"I love it." Derek curls his notebook. "I'll tell you, if you did it, you'd make your name at Bryan, that's for sure!"

"Yeah!" I say again, gathering courage.

"You'd be the most popular freshman in the school," Laura says reflectively. "Of course, you'd have to move to Alaska, but we could fax you your fan mail."

Derek belches for emphasis. "It's crazy, but I do love it. I just love it."

Suddenly I realize what I've said. "Maybe . . . maybe it is crazy. Too crazy."

Derek shakes his head. "No. It's not that crazy. It's kind of . . . brilliant, actually. And I'd love to help."

Laura nods. "Me too!"

My heart flutters. "Help?"

Derek leans against the wall by an elbow. "Sure. If you want. Of course, we'd have to do a fair, decent, honest article."

"Count me in too," Michael says.

I look at them. "Gee, you guys, that's great! But would Jeremy even print it?"

Laura smacks her lips. "For sure. He says he needs this article. Besides, you're only going to write the truth. Maybe you'll find out Frack's a saint."

I honk. Everybody else laughs—normally.

Opening a notebook, I begin jotting down "make list of kids who've had Frack; graduates too."

Michael looks over my shoulder and reads. "Good."

"My best friend's mom went to Bryan a long time ago. Maybe I'll talk to her," I say, closing the book.

I barely remember my best friend's face, but what the heck.

Laura smiles. "You all want to come over to my house Saturday night, and we can get organized?"

Everybody says "Great!" at once as I accidentally

glance at my watch. "Uh oh . . . I gotta go. Detention." I grin.

I can't believe what's happening to me.

"We'll walk you to the staircase," Michael says.

He moves up next to me, as Derek moves up next to Laura. Then, heading for the fourth floor doors, Derek moves around next to me, leaving Michael next to Laura.

I wonder if Derek likes Laura. Or if Laura likes Derek. Or if Michael likes Laura.

I wonder who I like the best.

It's confusing. But it doesn't matter because I feel great.

Yesterday, I had nothing to look forward to.

But today, I'm headed for a little excitement.

And yesterday I was alone. But now—I'm practically a crowd.

# Chapter 10

The moment I get home and put the key in the lock, I hear the phone ring. I fumble to unlock the door, but the more I fumble, the more it sticks. Finally, the key whooshes around and I make a dash for the phone.

"Molly?" It's Kathy.

"Hi!" I answer. I switch the receiver into the other hand, lift the long extension wire and head for the living room.

"How ya doin'?" I think for a second. "How was the student council meeting?"

"Scary. But fabulous."

"Really? How so?" I turn around and head for the fridge. While I'm talking, some milk would be nice.

"Well, everybody was so . . . so rich. So cool. You know who ran the meeting? Kevin Blake, the mayor's son! And you know who's recording secretary? Nicole Beauchamp who lives in that mansion on Exeter Street that always scared us. She lives there winters. She spends summers in her French château! And she likes me!"

"How . . . nice."

"Yeah. And would you believe, I'm invited to the mayor's house for a party Saturday. Is that great or what?"

"Or what . . . I mean, that's great."

"Me! Can you imagine. Mayor Blake is in the *Verona Times* every day. And I am going to sit on his couch!"

"Yeah. He was just in the paper. For graft, I think."

"So? It's exciting. I'm even invited to Andrea Durmack's house. Her father is the third richest orthodontist in the state, Nick says. I mean really. . . So, you want to come Saturday to meet the mayor? I bet I can get you invited. These kids are actually nice."

I open the refrigerator door. No milk. "I'm supposed to go over to this girl's house. Somebody who's working on the *Bugle* with me . . ."

"The *Bugle*? You made it already?"

"No. But I'm working on a story, a real investigative piece. And I met some kids who might help me. Derek Anderson, for one."

"Derek? I always liked him. Except for his belching and other . . . body noises."

"He's so cute now."

"No kidding. Hey, that's terrific. Well, you want to come?"

"Kathy, I said I was busy."

86

"Right. Sorry. I just thought you'd enjoy it."

"It looks like St. Bart's turned out to be a great school for you. You're . . . fitting in beautifully."

Another brilliant subtle insult.

"I'm trying," Kathy says. "How about Wednesday? Come over Wednesday after school. Maybe I could get Kevin Blake to come over. You could date the mayor's son."

"I have no desire to date a mayor's son," I say, thinking this for the first time. "Power corrupts. And the son of a powerful person is absolutely corrupt."

"Huh?"

I may not understand my oldest friend anymore, but I seem to be espousing some new principles.

"Well, maybe you could come over anyway," she says, a little coolly.

"Maybe. Will your mom be there? I need to talk to her about whether she knows this teacher, Henry Frack."

"Wait a sec." I hear a muffled conversation and then Kathy says, "My mom thought he was dead."

"He is," I say. "But I have him for history. Will she be there?"

"Yeah."

"Great. Then, I'll definitely see you Wednesday."

"Oh. Well, fine," Kathy answers coldly. "I . . . look forward to it. Bye."

And we both hang up together.

Even the dial tone sounds a little distant.

I dial information, then Verona Hospital, and ask for my mom's room.

"Mom? It's me."

"Hi, honey," Her voice sounds soft and gentle. I feel like I haven't spoken to her in a long time, even though I just saw her this morning.

"How are you feeling?"

"Well, considering . . . I'm feeling fine."

"Considering? Considering what?"

There is silence. "Considering I'm feeling lousy." She laughs one of those laughs that aren't really funny. I don't know what to say.

"Listen, Molly, there are individual beef stews in the freezer that you can put in the microwave."

"Okay."

"And also, I hid two frozen brownies behind the ice cubes. One for you and one for Billy. Make sure you get yours."

"Okay. Let me see if I can find them." Putting the phone under my chin, I open the freezer and dig around in the back. "Found 'em," I say.

"Good."

"Mom, these kids I like and I, we're working on the newspaper together." I sit down again. "And we're having a party Saturday. Isn't that great? One of them's Derek Anderson. You know him. He lives in Home Acres."

"Sure. Isn't he the boy who used to throw Matchbox cars off the porch and hit people?"

"Uh . . . yeah. But he's changed. I like him a lot. I like everybody." I take a slow sip of sweet peach soda. Just thinking about my group makes me feel good.

"That's wonderful, honey," my mom is saying. "I knew Bryan would work out. And how's school itself. You know, marks, grades, homework?" She laughs.

"Okay. I have a Latin quiz tomorrow. I'm going to study real hard because I didn't do as well as I wanted on the first quiz."

"Oh. What did you get?"

"Uh . . . eighty-two." I just can't say the word *forty-four* to my mother.

"Well," she says. "You just want to boost that up a little to a ninety. Right?"

"I think I can do that." I put down the glass. "So, how are you feeling? Are you going to stay a few days . . ."

There's another silence.

"What's the matter, Mom?"

"Molly . . ."

"Mom, please. Tell me."

There is another silence.

"Mom, what?"

"Molly, I . . . I didn't come into the hospital for pneumonia. I know I shouldn't have lied, but I thought it would turn out to be nothing."

I don't say a thing.

"I had found . . . there was . . . a lump. And I . . . it's been going on for a while. That's why I went to see a doctor. And had it x-rayed. I came in today for a biopsy. And . . . they found something."

89

"Found something? Where?"

"My breast." Her voice is barely audible.

"Oh." I sink back against the kitchen chair. "I didn't know that. Nobody told me that . . ." I say weakly.

"They're very optimistic. It was small, and they found it early. But . . ." Her voice sounds trembly. "They're doing some . . . some exploratory surgery tomorrow, to see the extent of it."

"I'm coming to the hospital, Mom. I'm coming right over!"

"No, honey. Don't!"

"Yes! I'm coming."

"Molly, please. I don't want you to!" Her voice is urgent for a second, and then it softens into her other, sweeter voice. "They're going to give me medication to get a good night's sleep. I'm tired. But I love you. Very very much."

"I love you too, Mom."

"I'll see you soon."

"Tomorrow?"

"Maybe. Now, you've got a Latin test. Study."

"Study?"

"Please, for me. And go to school. And call me tomorrow as soon as you get home, okay?"

"Okay."

"Good girl." And she hangs up.

I walk back to my dad's easy chair and sink into the cushions. I just sit there for a while and then pick up my Latin book. *Our Latin Tradition.*

I stare at it, trying to concentrate. My hands are shaking.

It had been such a good day. Now, it was such an awful day. How can that be?

I shouldn't have insisted that I go to the hospital. I upset her.

I think back to the moment before I called. I wish I could take that phone call back. I wish I didn't know. I wish it weren't true.

Breast cancer. What did that mean? What would they do to her. My mom. My perfect mom.

The main thing is that she be okay. And, she said it was a tiny lump. So tiny, she said, that they could barely detect it.

But they did detect it.

I have this horrible thought. Usually I'm so good. So obedient. But lately, I've been . . . not so good. Maybe it's my fault. Maybe I caused this.

I know that's crazy. It has to be crazy.

I look at the cover of my Latin book. A picture of some Roman gladiators against a strong blue Roman sky. I open the book again. Covering the Latin words, I look at the English and recite their Latin meanings out loud.

I look over at the sentences I have to translate into Latin. "The boy and the girl and the farmer are with the sailor."

I throw the book across the living room.


For the next two hours, I walk around the house, turn on the tv for a little while, then turn it off. I make some chocolate pudding, then look at my homework, then go back to the tv. On one turn of the dial, I pass one of those television evangelists. He is telling the audience how to be saved. I flip off the set, and kneel on the carpet.

"Please, please God, I'll do anything. Anything you want."

Then I go to the phone and dial Kathy's number, but there's no answer. Just as I hang up, the phone rings.

"Hello, Molly? This is Derek."

"Hi."

"I have some great news. I spoke to Charlie about Frack. He wants to talk to us."

"That's . . . great."

"Molly . . . is . . . is something wrong?"

"Uh huh . . ." I feel tears in my eyes and my voice is trembling.

"What's the matter?" Derek asks.

"Everything."

I can't help it. I start to cry.

"Molly, you want me to come over?"

"Gee. I . . . yeah. I would."

"I'll be right there."

# Chapter 11

"Hi." I meet Derek at the kitchen door. "Come on in."

"What's wrong?" he asks.

We sit down at the kitchen table.

I lean my elbow on a placemat and cover my eyes.

Then I shake my head. "My mom . . . she's sick."

"Gee. Very sick?"

I nod.

"Is it . . ." He hesitates. "What is it?"

I lower my eyes. I make myself say the word. "It's cancer."

But just saying it, I feel my shoulders start to tremble, and then I can't help it, they begin to heave and the tears and the sobs pour out.

Derek just sits there. Occasionally I look up at him, embarrassed, but then I start crying again.

Finally I raise my head and try to shake away the tears.

"I'm sorry," he says. "I really am." He puts his hand on the table an inch from mine.

"You can cry more. I don't mind," he says.

I shake my head. "I'm finished. I'm pretty sure."

We stare at each other for a few seconds.

"I'm sorry I made you come over."

"Hey, that's okay."

"You want a brownie or something?"

"Sure."

I go to the back of the refrigerator and retrieve the two brownies as I calm down. For a second I worry my brother will kill me for not saving one, but I put them in the microwave anyway, then bring them to the table.

Derek takes a bite, then says, "Your mom made these, right?"

I nod.

He takes another bite. "She's really nice too. I remember I once dropped a Matchbox truck on her head when she passed our porch. And she took it very well." He grins.

"She loves toys," I answer, smiling. "And kids."

My eyes are getting watery again.

He reaches over to pat my hand, and then gets up and peeks through the arch that leads to the living room. "You know, people can be all right with cancer. My parents know a few people like that. What kind does she have?"

I don't want to say it. "A bad kind."

"I thought so." He walks into the living room, and then back to the kitchen. "I see you have a piano. You play?"

I get up too. "Not really. Billy and I both took lessons for a while. We were both pretty bad."

"Mind if I . . ." He walks to the living room and I follow. Sitting down on the bench, he lifts the cover and taps out a few notes.

"Nice piano . . . nice sound."

"Thanks. My mom got it on sale." I take a deep breath.

"Would you mind if I play something?"

"No. I'd like that."

He sits up straighter, cracks his knuckles and grins. "Sorry." Then he wiggles his fingers over the keys. "I just learned this. So far, it's probably cost my parents about three hundred dollars." He looks up at me again. "It's Beethoven's Sonata Number Eight. This is the slow movement. It's real pretty."

He begins to play.

The tune is so soft and pretty but it also seems so sad that the tears come to my eyes again.

"That bad, ay," Derek says, looking up at me.

I shake my head. "No. I really like it."

Actually, it's beautiful. As Derek plays, I can't help staring at his profile. He's not handsome because he has a very bumpy nose. But his eyes are so deep set and blue and intense that I think he's cute anyway.

Even if he's just going to be my friend, he's a very cute friend.

He finishes with loud, dramatic chords and then looks up at me. "Would you pay three hundred dollars for that?"

"At least." I grin.

He pats the stool next to him and I sit down.

I am aware of his body so close to mine.

"You play chopsticks?" he asks.

"But of course. That's all I can remember."

He plays the right hand. I play the left.

We play it fast and then faster and then faster until it turns into just plain noise.

The louder it sounds, the better it makes me feel.

Suddenly, the phone rings and startles us.

I slide off the bench, run to the kitchen and pick up the receiver. It's Derek's father. They want him home.

Derek puts on his jacket. As I walk him to the kitchen door, I hear my dad's car pulling into the driveway, and then the front door slams.

Derek opens the screen and we walk along the hedge.

"Are you going to school tomorrow?" he asks.

"I guess . . . I promised I would."

"Well, if you feel like it, Charlie said he could meet us at Vinnie's Pizza right after school and tell us what he knows. I mean, if you feel like it."

I bite my lip. I think of my mom, and of coming home to an empty house. "Okay. That would be good."

"Great." Derek puts his arms on my shoulders, presses down a little and then pats them. "I'm really sorry about your mom."

"I know. And thanks. Thanks a lot."

I watch him as he jogs across our lawn toward his block and then I walk back inside.

96

As soon as I enter the kitchen, Billy yells at me.

"Is that all the brownies?"

I shrug. "I'm sorry. I had company."

"I'm starved."

"There's beef stew," I offer.

He shakes his head. "Wasn't that Derek Anderson?"

"Yes."

"Isn't he the kid who released fifty baby crablets at the Whitman Junior High lunchroom a couple of years ago?"

"He's changed." I slice off the chewed edges of my bitten brownie, forming a perfect but tiny minibrownie. "You could have this. I hardly ate it."

He takes it and swallows it in one gulp.

We just stand there for a while.

"Dad told me . . ." he begins. "He picked me up after track."

"Where is he?"

"At the corner store. He dropped me off and went for some groceries."

"She said it's just . . . tiny," I begin, but he looks at me like I don't know anything.

"It isn't good, that's for sure."

Just then the screen door whooshes open again and my father walks in, carrying a bag full of groceries.

"Hi, kids," he says, almost enthusiastically. "Somebody want to help me with this?"

Billy takes the bag from my dad's arms and puts it on the table. I inspect it, take out the cartons of milk and juice and head for the refrigerator.

97

"You want some coffee, Dad? Or some chocolate pudding?"

"Chocolate pudding," Billy says. "Why didn't you offer that to me?"

I ignore him as my father pats me on the back. "That would be good, Molly. I'm a little tired. I—I have to be at the hospital early, but I'd love some."

"How's Mom?" I ask, walking to the fridge.

"She's okay . . . she's okay."

I put a chocolate pudding on the table. "Is she in any pain?"

My father smiles. "Absolutely not."

I don't really want to ask any more questions. I don't want to know. But my father goes on. "Look, Molly. Billy. Everything is going to be okay. We have the best surgeon. The best. I'm sure they got it in time. We're very lucky."

Billy is frowning.

"Dr. Emory Fitzgerald," my father continues. "He's excellent. He assured us that there are plenty of options even if they find . . . more. Which the odds are against. So there's no need to worry."

Billy is just standing there.

"Billy, did you do your homework?"

"I just got home, Dad."

"Well, I want you both to do your work. Go to school. And I'll call you at three. You know we worry, but most of our worries never happen. It's always darkest before the dawn. Science is making a lot of progress. There's every reason to . . ."

My brother looks at me. I see anger in his eyes.

98

". . . be optimistic. You know your mother's being strong, and we have to be . . ."

Billy explodes. "God damn it, Dad! She's sick! She's *sick*, Dad. Stop that crap. It doesn't help."

He looks at Billy, surprised. "Raising your voice won't help either."

"Maybe it doesn't help you, but it helps me!" Billy shouts back.

I can't believe they're going to argue now. Of all times.

"Billy, please. Lower your voice or go to your room."

Billy nods. "Right. Go to your room. That's your answer to everything." His voice trembles. "God, what if anything happens to her? We'd be goddamn stuck with . . ."

And he heads for his room and slams the door.

My father looks at me, then looks away, but I can see tears are coming to his eyes.

I hear a door open, and then my brother walks out again. Head down, he goes straight for the refrigerator.

As he walks back past me, with a chocolate pudding, my father calls after him.

"I'm sorry, Billy. I'm sorry, son." His voice cracks. "I'm so, so sorry."

My brother turns around and stares at my father. His face softens and he nods.

I wish they would hug each other or something. But I guess they can't.

# Chapter *12*

I played hooky again. Partial hooky, actually, because I just couldn't make myself go to school.

I cut homeroom, but went in for my Latin test. I got a twelve.

Then I went home and took a nap.

And then I went back for Frack's class because I didn't want to have to bring in another absent note.

It turned out Frack wasn't there. He's at a three-day Teachers' Conference. It's probably entitled "Advanced Techniques in Not Teaching History."

Now I'm standing in front of Vinnie's Pizza, waiting for Derek and Charlie.

It's chilly, but I have to keep my raincoat open because when I close it, it catches on my tights. It's not painful, but separating Velcro from tights is noisy. I hope that when my mom comes home, she'll cut off the Velcro.

Here come Derek and Charlie.

I wave and they both wave back.

As we walk into Vinnie's, Derek says, "You two find empty seats. I'll get the pizza."

I follow Charlie to a back table still covered with pizza crusts and crumpled tomato stained napkins.

He casually shoves everything against the wall, raises one leg over the back of the chair, and sits down.

"Derek tells me you're going to write about Frack for the newspaper," he says immediately. "It's a great idea but you better be careful."

I cover the pizza crusts with some napkins. "I'll be careful," I say. "And maybe I won't. Who cares, anyway?"

"Not that Frack doesn't deserve whatever he gets. He's the worst. What are you going to write about?"

"I don't know. Depends on the stories we get."

He plays with a napkin. "Right. See, the thing is, I don't want Derek to get into too much trouble. He's just a freshman. And I'm trying to guide him. I don't want him to make the same mistakes I did."

"Well, gee. That's nice, Charlie. But only my name is going on the article. So if anyone is going to get into trouble, it'll be me."

As I say this, I know I sound brave. But I don't really feel it. I feel like a part of me is acting bold and daring, while the real me is saying, "Don't worry, you never get into trouble. I'll tell you when to chicken out."

I smile appreciatively at Charlie. "Anyway, it's nice that you're so . . . protective."

"Yeah. I know." He squeezes the napkin, and throws it back on the table.

I grin. "My brother's protective of me too. At least, he was once. In 1983."

Charlie laughs as Derek walks over with two cardboard trays balanced precariously in his hands.

"I have three slices here, pepperoni, pepperoni and pepperoni," he says, standing cheerfully before us. "What kind would you like, Molly?"

"Uh—let me think . . ."

Charlie raises himself by his big arms and leans his big bulldog face over the platter of slices to get a better look. He points to the biggest piece. "That one," he says.

Derek hands it to him, then sits in the chair next to mine and distributes the Cokes. I hand him my money and he slips it in his jacket pocket.

I can't wait until the day when a boy cares about me enough, cherishes me enough, to pay for my pizza.

"So, did you tell Molly anything about Frack?" Derek asks, counting my change.

"I was about to," Charlie says. He folds his pizza, tilts it, and bites off an enormous piece. When the pizza emerges from his mouth, there's not much left.

"Garlic. Red pepper," he orders.

Derek reaches across the table and hands them over.

"Thanks. So, Molly, this is the scoop." He bites again. We wait again. "Everyone—the teachers, the principal, the chairman of the social studies department—knows that Frack is bad. And there's a rumor that they tried to get him to transfer or retire but he refused. So they compromised and he only teaches two classes. Unfortunately, you're two of the poor suckers he still teaches."

"If everyone knows he's incompetent, why can't they just fire him?"

Charlie looks at me like I'm mentally handicapped. "Molly, incompetence is not sufficient cause for firing a teacher. You need something—unusual." We all laugh.

I think a second. "I could never write that they tried to force him to retire. I couldn't prove it."

Derek's eyes widen. "But if you could—now *that* would be a great story!"

"Eat your pizza, Derek," Charlie says.

"On the other hand," I continue, "I could write that he only teaches two classes. That's an interesting fact. I'll bet he's getting his whole salary for two courses." I take a bite of my pizza.

"I'll bet," Derek says, sipping his Coke. "Anyway, that's good. What else, Charlie?"

A lone strand of cheese connects Charlie's thumb to his pizza. He stretches and stretches it, 'til it breaks. Then he swallows the strand. "Well, he's a very unfair marker. You know how many smart kids go to summer school."

I nod nervously.

"Even good students flunk because he gives all these surprise quizzes. With trick questions."

We nod.

Charlie looks at Derek. "Do you know Randy Asaad?"

"Sure," Derek answers. "Genius. Pakistani. Great poker player."

"Yeah. Well, Frack hated Randy because he got all the trick questions right. Randy got everything right, but he fell asleep in class a couple of times. Who doesn't? Frack gave him zeros each time—and a sixty on the final essay exam. So Randy got a fifty-five in the course. The kid has a ninety-five average and Frack flunked him. It's outrageous."

"Wow. Can I call Randy?"

"Sure," Charlie says. "I'll get you his number. Anyway, that gives you some idea of the way the Hack marks. Plus, he tells you the final grades. You never get your exams back because he uses them over and over."

"Did you have him?" I ask.

"Uh huh. I barely passed myself. Luckily, I got great homeworks from a kid on the wrestling team."

I look at him quizzically.

"Yeah, that's another thing. He's been giving the same homework assignments for thirty years too. They're long, but if you find a kid who did them . . ."

Derek looks over to me. "I'll give 'em to you if Charlie finds 'em."

"I'm looking, I'm looking. Hey, don't bug me. They cost me ten bucks, they go for thirty now and I'm giving them to you for cost." Charlie gobbles up his remaining pizza like a bear, but then very gently brushes his fingers against each other.

"Well, I hope you nail him." He throws down his napkin. "I gotta go."

Waving good-bye to us, he heads for the door.

Derek pushes back his chair. "I guess I ought to go too. Piano lessons. Are you heading home, Molly?"

"Yes. My dad's supposed to call."

"I think you got some good stuff from Charlie."

"Definitely. And I'm seeing my friend's mother later. She said she had great stories too."

"Molly, this is going to be dynamite!"

"If only I knew who was going to blow up." I grin.

He does too. "Would you mind if I call you later?"

"That'd be nice."

"I told Michael and Laura about your mom. Was that okay?"

My hands move instinctively to cover my face.

"I guess it wasn't," he says.

"I just don't want everybody to know. Just them, okay?"

"Right."

Derek puts out his hand to pull me up from my seat.

"Thanks," I say.

I walk in front of him and then wriggle past two tables of kids who smile at us. As we walk out the door, he gently puts his hand on my back.

It's not quite as good as having your pizza paid for, but I think it's a step in the right direction.

105

When I get home, Billy is already there.

He makes us some hot chocolate and we sit at the kitchen table, waiting for my father's call.

"Did you play hooky?" I ask him as he plops a marshmallow on top of my steaming cup.

"Nope. I was going to but I had this great idea. And it kept my mind busy so I went to Bryan."

"What? Tell me."

He smiles. "I got Dad's label maker, and I made my name about twenty times. Then I broke into the trophy case, and put Billy Snyder labels on each and every trophy."

My mouth drops for a second, and then I start to giggle. Then honk.

"That's great, Billy. That's so great!" I stare at him. "You know, you're so . . . creative. You're like Mom. More than me."

That is so nice of me to admit, I can't believe I'm saying it.

"Thanks," he says. "You are too. You're like Dad though. Smart. Disciplined. Into justice." He grins. "Those aren't such terrible qualities."

The phone rings.

Billy snatches it up in a second.

I run for the extension.

"Kids . . . it's Dad. Everything's under control."

"Is she . . . okay?" Billy asks.

"She's asleep. She's . . . asleep."

I take a deep breath and ask, "What happened?"

My father speaks so softly I can barely hear him. "She's coming home Saturday. Uh . . . they're not

106

sure. They want to do a few more tests, and then it's up to Mom. She can think it over for a little while. But she'll need . . . some surgery. If you want, you can visit her tomorrow. She'd like that."

"Sure," we both say.

"They really are optimistic. Really." There's a long pause. "I have to go over to the office for a little while, but I love you both very much. Both of you . . . very much."

When Billy and I hang up, each still gripping a receiver, we stare at each other for a moment.

"What does it mean?" I ask softly.

Billy shrugs. "It means they have to decide," he doesn't look at me, "how much to cut. They let the woman—Mom—decide what she wants to do. A lumpectomy. Or a mastectomy."

I cringe. My mind is picturing my mother's body, and I can't stand it. I force myself to close my brain because it's making me feel the knife in my stomach. Billy pushes off from the table with his knuckles.

"I think I'll go over to Jim's for a little while. Is that okay?"

I shake my head. "Sure. I'm going over to Kathy's later."

"Good idea."

"Right." I *hope* seeing Kathy is a good idea.

After I watch my brother put on his leather jacket and leave, I go into my bedroom, put on my stereo earphones, turn up the music as loud as I can bear it, which is pretty loud, and take my second nap of the day.

# Chapter 13

Before I have a chance to knock on the Marantzes' front door tonight, Mrs. Marantz is there to greet me.

I follow her into the hall, and down three little steps to their sunken living room.

The Marantzes' have the nicest house in our development. There are big comfortable sofas in the living room, a red Persian rug and a grand piano. Glass doors lead out to a new gray wood patio that's filled with wicker furniture and hanging plants.

"Come on in, Molly dear," Mrs. Marantz waves me inside. "Would you like something to drink?"

I nod. She opens the little refrigerator under the bar, and I peek in and choose a French raspberry soda, which she pours into a tall thin frosted glass.

Even the drinks in the Marantz house could be in a decorating magazine.

I go to one of the sofas and plop down into a soft cushion as Princess jumps up next to me.

Mrs. Marantz looks at me sympathetically. "I spoke to your dad. Janie will be home from the hospital Friday or Saturday, right?"

I nod. "I'm going to visit her tomorrow," I mumble and then pet Princess, who licks my face.

Mrs. Marantz seems about to say something else about my mom so I change the subject.

"Is Kathy home yet?" I ask.

I don't know why, but even with Mrs. Marantz, I just don't want to talk about my mom. Maybe because I know it's not going to make me feel good.

She shakes her head, studies me for a second and then smiles. "So, how about some cookies? I have chocolate lace, oatmeal raisin and Chocolate Lido cookies. Let me get them." She heads for the kitchen as I pull out my notebook.

On the way back, Mrs. Marantz looks at her watch. "Kathy went somewhere with Nick, but she should be back in fifteen minutes. At the latest. Is that enough time to talk to me about Henry Frack?"

"I think so," I say.

"Good." Mrs. Marantz brings the little tray of cookies up to me and I take an oatmeal raisin.

"So," she begins, "what do you want to know?"

"Well, I wanted you to tell me about Frack in the old . . . back when you went to school."

"Right. Well, I have been thinking about it, actually and uh, I wasn't crazy about the man."

"No one is."

"I'd have to say—I hated him."

"You did?" I ask happily, and then try to show sympathy. "I mean, that's a shame."

I glance at the questions I've written down in advance. First, I ask some background questions: the exact years she went to Bryan, her maiden name, what course she took in high school, where she lived, that kind of thing.

I write everything down in a big scribble. I hope I can read it later!

Then I look up. "Okay. Now, what years did you have Frack? Freshman, like me?"

Mrs. Marantz leans back against the sofa and nods. "I had him freshman year *and* senior year. When I got him senior year, I was pretty sure God was punishing me for something." She grins. "Frack was *mean* and I mean *mean!*"

I try to sound professional. "Can you explain just what you mean by *mean*, if you know what I mean?"

We both laugh. "Sure," she says. "I mean he'd scream at you and you never knew what you did. I mean he gave six-page homework assignments which took two hours. I mean, you'd have a problem—a real problem—and he'd ignore you. Like kids weren't people."

I nod. "That's it exactly. He treats us like we're not people."

Mrs. Marantz takes a chocolate lace cookie and begins nibbling. "He assumed we didn't want to learn, which wasn't true at all!"

"That is so true. That is so true!"

110

Mrs. Marantz looks at me nervously. "Molly, does your dad know you're doing this?"

I shake my head. "I'll tell him eventually."

"Maybe I should call him. I don't want to get you into trouble."

"Mrs. Marantz, I'm an investigative reporter. I know what I'm doing. Anyway, my father has always taught me to have courage, to be true to myself, that if I worked hard, I could make a difference in this world."

"You sure he doesn't just mean cleaning your room?" Mrs. Marantz begins chuckling to herself and can't stop. "Sorry. Look, I think you're great. I'm not worried about you. In fact, I wish Kathy were more interested in school and less interested in . . . her new social life."

I swallow nervously. "She seems to love St. Muffy's. I mean St. Bart's."

"I guess so. But you were always a good influence. You made her study."

"Well, she's very busy. It's good that she's made good friends." Gosh. I'm such a liar. Anything to seem like a nice person.

"Anyway, what else? Can you remember any specific times that Frack was mean and how it affected you?"

She nods silently. "Many. But, there was one time . . . that was a little worse."

I look at her as professionally as possible. "Yes?"

"It's embarrassing."

"You can tell me."

She scrunches up her chin. "Well . . ."

111

"Have another cookie," I say.

Smiling, she takes a bite, then gulps her French fruit drink. "It was freshman year." She studies a picture on the wall.

"Freshman year. Right," I say.

She bounces a finger against her lip as though she's deciding whether to confess. Then she goes on. "Anyway, he always gave us surprise quizzes, but around the fifth week of school, he gave us a surprise midterm!" She shakes her head. "It was a total shock because among other things, he hadn't taught us anything. He just gave us handouts."

I scribble furiously.

"Plus, he said the test would count for *half* of our first report card. So I got nervous immediately. And, when I saw the exam, I—I just froze. I'd think of one answer, then another, but my mind was racing." She wrinkles her nose. "I panicked and didn't write a thing. I handed in a totally blank test paper!"

"How awful."

"Wait. That was the good part. A couple of days later, he's sitting at the head of the class and he looks like he's in ecstasy. And he tells us that he's going to read our grades out loud and comment on our papers!"

"Oh, gee," I say sympathetically.

Mrs. Marantz gets up. "I need another cookie." She sandwiches two together and takes a major bite. "Anyway, he starts reciting our marks, row by row. Some kids did okay. But when he got to a kid who didn't, he'd say something sarcastic. I started to get more and more upset as he got to my row. It was like a cold sweat." She looks at me. "And I think I'm feeling it again."

"Gee, Mrs. Marantz, if it's too painful, you don't have to tell it."

"No. That's okay." She plunks the rest of the double cookie into her mouth. "Too bad I'm not a drinking woman. This would be a good time for a martini!" She grins at me. "Anyway, he was up to the kid in front of me. Reading my zero to the entire class was seconds away. Seconds. So I did the only thing I could think of. Just before he got to my name, I grabbed my stomach, slid off my seat and moaned."

My eyes open a little wider. I try not to laugh.

"Frack looked at me in a panic. He hated scenes. But I moaned again and," she shakes her head, "then I shouted 'Appendix!' from below the desk . . ."

I can't help it. I laugh.

Luckily, so does she. "It's funny now. But it wasn't funny then. Not only did they call the nurse, but I overdid it so much that they also called an ambulance. It was last period, and there I was, outside Bryan High School, kids pouring out, sitting in a wheelchair. They covered my knees with a blanket and everything."

"Gee," I say. "Poor kid."

She nods. "I'll never forget it. I kept whispering to the nurse, 'You know, I think I feel a little better,' but it was too late."

"They took you to the hospital?"

"Uh huh. Luckily my mom came, took one look at me and knew something was fishy."

"Wow."

Princess is now at her feet, concerned. Mrs. Marantz pets her. "I can feel the anger rising again. I really can."

"Mrs. Marantz, why do they allow teachers like him?"

Princess jumps up and puts her head in Mrs. Marantz's lap. "I don't know, Molly. Every school has a Mr. Frack." Gently moving Princess, she stands up. "God, I'm glad I'm grown up and just have to worry about my job, my daughter and finding a new husband." She grins.

I get up too. "I'd like to use this if I can. Would you mind?"

"I . . . I guess not." Her eyes become thoughtful. "You know, when you look back as an adult, it does seem almost funny and unimportant. But Frack was important to me then. He gave me nightmares. And I never forgot him. He didn't like kids. He was incompetent and . . . sadistic."

I write that down in capital letters.

Mrs. Marantz stands up. "Be careful, Molly. Be smart. But, well, if you need me, call, okay?"

"Thanks," I say, starting to feel excited. "Actually, all I need now is some biography stuff. Teaching facts. That kind of thing."

Mrs. Marantz fluffs her wild blond hair. "You know Flo Garfield? She's head of the PTA at Bryan. She might know something. You want me to call her?"

"Sure."

"Okay." Mrs. Marantz moves closer to me. "And when you talk to Janie . . . to your mom, tell her I'll call her at the hospital tomorrow, okay, with some more information about the lumpectomy procedure."

I swallow because as soon as I hear that word, and think of my mother and what she's got, my eyes get a little watery again and my mouth feels soft and trembly.

Mrs. Marantz looks at me gently, but I can't help it. My throat closes and I feel the tears coming.

"Molly . . . Molly, I know . . . I know." Mrs. Marantz is walking toward me as the phone rings. She touches my shoulder gently and heads for the kitchen.

Picking up the phone, her face immediately turns into a frown. "Why? That's ridiculous. We're waiting . . . You're impossible." She shakes her head. "No, you tell her." Mrs. Marantz hands the phone over to me. "It's Kathy. She's stuck."

I take the receiver and listen.

"I'm sorry, Molly. I really am. I can't believe Nick's bad luck. His Jaguar broke down. We're stuck on Shore Boulevard . . ."

I'm so upset I can't believe it, but I interrupt and say just the opposite. "Hey look, these things happen. You know, Jaguars aren't perfect . . . No problem. Actually, I mostly needed to interview your mom. Which I did."

"I figured that," she says coldly.

Which makes the tears come to my eyes.

115

Mrs. Marantz interrupts on the extension. "Molly's been here for a while, Kathy. And she has a few things on her mind . . . that she needed a friend for."

I put up my hand for Mrs. Marantz to stop. Hanging up the receiver, I hear her on the other line, telling Kathy about my mom. I pick up key phrases even though I don't want to listen. "Breast cancer." "Lumpectomy." "Mastectomy." "You should have been here."

Instead of making me feel better, it makes me feel worse.

When Mrs. Marantz hangs up, though, she takes my hands.

"I'm sorry, Molly. She didn't know." Frowning at first, she then smiles sheepishly. "She's never home . . . and I miss her too."

As I nod, Mrs. Marantz folds me into her arms. And even though nothing's going to make me feel better except knowing for sure that my mother will be okay, it feels good, so good, to be held.

# Chapter 14

A guard opens the door at Verona Hospital, and a woman at an information desk tells us to take Elevator Bank C to the sixth floor.

As I walk down the corridor, I try not to look too closely at the patients, people with pale white skin leaning weakly against silver metal walkers, or slumped in wheelchairs. I hate the IV's that hang on hooks and lead to skinny tubes attached to their arms.

I hope my mom doesn't look like that.

I hope she doesn't have anything up her nose.

Billy stops a nurse. "Can you tell me where Room 632C is, please?"

She smiles cheerfully. Too cheerfully. "Sure. It's down the hall, through those doors, and then it's the second door on the left. Easy as pie!"

"Thank you," we both murmur, and give each other a look. I know what Billy's thinking: How can anybody be so cheerful in a hospital?

We push open the double doors, spot the little metal plate that says 632C and walk into the large room.

A very old woman in the first bed has tubes in her nose and is snoring softly.

My mom waves from a corner bed.

As soon as I see her, hooked up to one of those intravenous things, the breath goes right out of me. I smile weakly.

I couldn't wait to see my mom, but now that I'm here, I feel scared.

Billy gives her a kiss, and then, standing on line behind him, I do too. Naturally, he immediately takes the only guest chair. I stand awkwardly until she pats the edge of her bed and says, "Sit down, Molly."

Her face seems so pale, and her hair is a little straggly.

"So, how're you feeling, Mom?" Billy asks in an upbeat voice.

She tries to smile. "Okay."

I feel shy and I don't know what to say.

"You look great," I lie. That was pretty stupid.

"Thanks." My mom's eyes seem so sad that I have to look away. And I hate to see her in that hospital gown.

I wish I could say something that would cheer her up but I feel so formal, so uncomfortable in this stupid place.

"Do you need anything?" Billy stands up, and I immediately slide over to take the chair. "I could get you something to drink. Like a Coke."

She wipes her lips with her tongue. "Sure. That would be great, Billy. There's a little luncheonette counter on the first floor. I'd love a Sprite actually."

"It's yours!"

Billy gets up and walks out, leaving my mom and me alone. We sit there quietly for a minute until she points to the end table and bureau. "Lots of flowers."

"Pretty." I point to some roses. "Those are beautiful. And those too."

I feel proud that so many people care about my mom.

Her arms stretch out toward me so I get up again, go to her and clasp them. She tries to smile but it's a sad smile. "Listen, Molly, I want you to understand what's happening. I don't want you to worry."

"Worry? Me?"

She laughs softly.

"Well, it's . . . it's upsetting. And I guess I'm a little depressed. I'm sorry."

"Hey, who wouldn't be depressed? I mean . . ."

She laughs again. "That's okay. I just want you to understand what's going on. All the results aren't back, but at first they thought they saw something suspicious in the lymph nodes. And now, there's less than they thought. There really is . . ." her eyes get watery, "there really is every reason to be optimistic."

"That's good!"

She nods. "They tell me that once they get it all

119

out, it's out. And I'm going to be okay. There's a ninety-five percent chance I'm going to be totally fine." She smiles but you can't even see her dimples.

I squeeze her hand, and then I can't help it, I blurt out, "Will they remove your . . . will they . . ."

She looks away.

"I'm not sure. It's kind of up to me to decide." And she sighs.

Damn. I said the wrong thing again.

"You're . . . you're so pretty, Mom. No matter what."

"Thanks." Then, wrinkling her chin, she blurts out, "Some people say that you cause your own cancer. Maybe I did something. Maybe I . . . Damn, I'm so sorry to do this to you kids!"

"Mom! You're crazy!"

She grins. "Now that made me feel better."

"You know what I mean. You didn't cause it. We might have. Two teenagers is too much for any person."

"Two teenagers and Dad is why I want to get well." She shakes her head. "I'm sorry. I had planned what to say. That everything was going to be fine. That you shouldn't worry. I'm not handling this well."

I've never seen my mom like this. So . . . so shaky.

Lowering her eyes, she runs her fingers through the hair near her ears to calm down. "I just have to get a handle on this and then I'll be fine. I will."

120

She looks over to the bureau and picks up a sheet of paper. "Molly, do you mind? I have to ask you to call the grocery store and make sure they deliver."

She hands me a shopping list. "But there are still plenty of entrées you can . . ."

"Microwave."

"Exactly. But I'll be home soon, and then I'll get everything in order again. I will. Everybody's calling to tell me I'll be fine." She raises her eyebrows like she knows that those are just words. "And, Molly, be sure to talk to Dad. He'll be there for you."

My heart starts pounding. "What do you mean? You said you'll be home soon."

She shakes her head. "I know. I know. I just mean sometimes we treat Dad like, you know, you can't be honest with him. You can."

"Right."

She bites her lip. "You know, honey," her voice trembles, "I'm not . . . I've never been as perfect as you thought I was. And now if I have a mastectomy, I know you're worried, but . . . would you also be ashamed of me?"

"Mom . . ." She is so honest.

Her arms reach out to me again. "Hold me, Molly, okay? Just a little hug."

I hold her as tight as I can and brush away the hair from her face.

She looks up at me and smiles sheepishly. "You know, I only got to be really pretty in my twenties. I have freckles. I just hide them. I . . . it took me so long to think I looked just right, to feel just right about myself as a woman." She shakes her head, then blushes a little, embarrassed. "I don't know why I said that."

"Me neither," I say. "I don't care what happens, I think you're beautiful."

But that doesn't help because she starts to cry. And soon she's weeping.

I can't stand it so I stroke her hair and give her a peck on the cheek and say the only thing I can think of. "Mom, I like you just the way you are. I'll love you no matter what."

"Me too. I love you so much."

As she holds me tighter, I feel a mixture of things.

Scared, because I don't know what I'm doing.

And pleased that she trusts me and loves me so much. Sometimes, a kid like me never really believes that.

For a second, I even feel like I'm a grown-up and she's *my* child.

But that last feeling passes as Billy walks back into the room and I immediately think a weird kid idea again. Stroking my mom's hair, I say, "I love you too, Mom" just a little louder than I have to.

I can't miss a chance to make Billy jealous.

# Chapter 15

Every shirt and sweater I own is lying on my bed.

It's Saturday and I'm trying to figure out what to wear to Laura's house tonight.

The brown lambswool is too dirty and the green turtleneck seems to have shrunk while it was hanging in the closet. And I just can't wear my blue tank top.

I wish my mother were here to make some great suggestions, but she took the car and went for a ride.

Since coming home yesterday, my mom either takes naps or car rides or sits at the kitchen table, thinking. Whenever I walk in, she'll smile, but it's hard to talk because I always feel I'm interrupting a conversation she's having with herself. I understand that she just wants to be alone, but I'm not used to it.

Last night both my mother and father explained again that the cancer she has has a ninety-five percent cure rate. She'll probably have a lumpectomy, where they remove the tumor, and then radiation and then maybe chemotherapy.

Whenever she says that word, cancer, I see her mouth get quivery or her eyes get glassy. I feel a pain in my own chest.

Now, looking in the mirror at myself, I can't help wondering if I could get breast cancer too. It's a strange thought, worrying about losing something I don't even have yet. I feel selfish just thinking about myself when my mom's the one who's really sick.

Sometimes my brain is like a runaway car. It just keeps going no matter what I do.

I wish I had a key that could turn it off.

I take a deep breath, stare at my sweaters and blouses one more time and then toss them back in the bottom of my closet.

I could wear my royal blue sweater. It's not too tight and not too loose and it looks pretty good on me.

The only problem is that I wore it to school all day yesterday, and that included three hours in the dusty PTA office searching through old news-letters with Mrs. Garfield until I found a tiny arti-cle on Frack.

I try the sweater on and sniff my underarms.

It'll be okay.

I have another selfish thought: Why can't Mom think about me for just ten minutes. Two weeks ago, she would have hopped in the car, dashed to the mall, and bought me something, knowing this was such an important night. I can't help feeling a little angry at her.

God. That's disgusting.

How could I feel such a thing, think such a thing?

Sometimes I'm such a terrible person.

I look in the mirror again. If I put my hair up and wear dangly silver earrings, it'll be good enough.

Sighing, I pin up my hair with a tortoiseshell barrette and strike a slinky pose in the mirror.

Kathy does this all the time. Slinks her body one way and her head the other, or lowers her eyelids to half-mast when she talks to a boy. When I do these things, I feel like a Vanna White impersonator.

I put my hands on my hips, raise my chin and stare, with half-closed lids, at the mirror again. "Hey, there," I whisper throatily to my reflection, "don't I know you from somewhere. . ."

I stop. It's just too embarrassing.

On my mom's vanity table are about five types of perfume. I spray some Coco perfume on my wrists, down my sweater and under my arms before I resmell myself. Excellent. While I'm there, I stuff a few tissues in my bra too.

In the kitchen, my brother Billy and my father are in the middle of a little fight.

I walk between them to the coat rack.

My father is yelling. "Is it too much to ask with your mother sick, that you put a glass in the dishwasher? Is that too much to ask?"

Billy shakes his head. "I was about to . . ."

"Excuse me, guys. I'm going."

Ignoring me, my dad holds up a glass that must have been in my brother's room for a while. "About to? About to?" When he shakes the glass, the milk wobbles like jelly.

"Billy, if you live like a slob, you think like a slob! Unless you get your act together, you're not going to have an act at all."

"I'm sorry, okay?" Billy answers sullenly.

I squeeze between them, put on my raincoat and head out the door.

Suddenly, I feel for Billy. He does take a lot of junk from my father. And, occasionally, he doesn't deserve it.

I peek back through the screen door and look at my father. "Hey, Dad, you know that glass you're holding? It's mine. I left it in Billy's room. Sorry. Really." I smile apologetically, then slam the screen door and hurry down the alley.

Okay, maybe I'm selfish and thoughtless sometimes, but that was nice of me.

By the time I get to Laura's house, Derek and Michael are already there. The three of them have been shooting pool in the basement. Laura leads me downstairs and asks if I want to play for a while.

"Sure," I say. Unsnapping my coat near the corner closet, I manage one last sniff of my sweater.

It's a little heavy on the Coco, but okay.

Taking a pool cue from a rack near the table, I

126

walk right over to Derek who grins at me. Michael waves hello.

Hmm. Derek smells sweet too.

That's interesting. Either he likes one of us, or his shirt is dirty also.

Looking at Laura in her long khaki skirt and soft white sweater, I wonder which of us it is. She's very pretty.

Michael places all the billiard balls into a metal triangle which he then places on the green felt table.

"Who wants to break?" he asks.

Laura volunteers. "The break," Michael explains to me, "is the opening shot, Molly. The idea is to try to get one ball in and set up your next shots."

"I see," I say. Which I don't.

Whack! Laura smacks the pack so hard that a red ball goes into a pocket.

Even the boys are impressed.

She then hits four more balls into pockets.

Laura may be fragile and delicate looking, but she plays pool like a sergeant.

I can't decide if that makes her more or less sexy.

After she finally misses, Derek goes. He misses his first try and immediately asks Laura if the basement floor is on a slight slant.

Then it's Michael's turn. When the green ball drops into a corner pocket, he looks up at Laura for a reaction.

Hmm. That could mean something. He might like her.

On my turn, all I hit is the air and Derek offers to give me a lesson. He stands beside me, making suggestions that I don't understand, even though I'm pretty sure they're in English.

It helps a little. Very little. On my second try, I hit air that's slightly closer to the ball.

Michael pats me on the back. "That was a little better," he says encouragingly. "Really."

Derek grins at Laura. "You, on the other hand, have a gift."

Who likes who here? It's driving me crazy.

I try to hit the ball one more time, but almost poke a hole in the felt.

"Okay," I say. "Would it be a terrible thing if I went upstairs and made brownies. I mean, I believe in the right of women to be in the major leagues and everything, but does it have to be me?"

The boys groan. "Gee, we wanna play. This pool table is sooo great," Derek says.

Laura puts her cue stick down. "I'll go up with Molly. I play all the time. Besides, the pizza should be here any sec. We'll bring it down when it comes."

Derek looks at her gratefully. "Thanks."

I think Derek might love this pool table more than he could ever love any girl. It's just a hunch.

As Laura and I climb the stairs, we hear him curse again and mutter, "I'm telling you, there's either something wrong with the floor or this cue stick."

Why does that seem adorable to me?

128

In the kitchen, as Laura takes out a brownie mix from the cabinet, I muster up my courage.

"Laura, which one do you like best? Derek or Michael?"

She breaks two eggs into the mix. "Whoever likes me. But that's hard to tell."

"I know."

She pours in some milk from the container I just handed her from the fridge.

"I have an idea," she says. "Eggs."

I hand over three eggs from the refrigerator egg tray.

"What?" I ask.

"Well, I have those two plastic couches downstairs, right? When we go back, let's move all the chairs out of reach. You sit on one couch. I'll sit on the other. Then, we'll see where each of them sits."

I break the third egg into the mix. "Great idea! That is a *great* idea."

I like Laura so much. She's so intelligent.

She turns on the mixer. "Of course, you have such a good figure. Like a model. They'll probably both sit next to you. Then I'll die."

I laugh. "Me?" I say.

She nods and points to my chest.

Looking to my left, and then my right, I reach into my sweater and pull out the tissues from my bra.

Putting my tongue in my cheek, and looking at the ceiling, I grin. "Sexy is . . . as sexy does."

Laura laughs. "Wow. Maybe I should do that."

"Maybe. But not tonight. It would be a little fishy if you grew breasts while we were making the brownies. Give yourself a week."

Saying that makes us both giggle.

Even though for an instant, I think of my mother.

Luckily, the bell rings. The pizza man.

Downstairs, Laura and I slyly move the chairs away, as the boys set the table.

I feel like we're playing musical chairs.

But when we go upstairs to get the Cokes, and then return, both chairs are back. Sitting down, Laura says to me, right in front of them, "Maybe we'll try hypnosis," and we both start to giggle again. This makes Derek look at Michael with that "girls are so dumb" look.

We're not dumb. We're dumbfounded that boys are so slow!

Michael takes a bite of pizza and says, "So, are we ready or what?"

I nod, stand up and pound the coffee table with a pool cue.

"Hear-yee. Hear-yee. This meeting of the Future Bryan *Bugle* Editorial Staff is called to order."

Everyone grins but I realize immediately what we're all thinking. Maybe all of us won't make the paper.

"Yesterday," I go on, "I found a little article about Frack that was written twenty-five years ago. It's boring but it has a few facts which I need."

Taking the article out of my knapsack, I hold it up.

130

"I've interviewed most of the kids who have him this year, and I've talked to a grown-up psychologist who called him a sadist. And I called Randy Asaad and got a quote. Nobody said anything nice. But luckily, this article from twenty-five years ago says good things."

Michael claps his hands. "Excellent, Molly. You have to write something complimentary before you tell everyone what a weasel he is. That's good journalism. What does the article say?"

I pass the newsletter over to Michael, who looks at it briefly, then passes it along as I summarize.

"It was written years ago when he was appointed head of the social science research class. It says he went to Ohio State and graduated with honors. And he's got a Master's." I make a face. "I'm supposed to call Mrs. Garfield back. She's going to check if kids won any awards while he was head of research."

I look at my watch. It's too early.

"Anyway," I go on, "I even have a nice quote from Frack." Derek passes the article back to me and I find it. "He says, 'We study history so that we may understand the past, so that we may better understand the present.' Not bad."

Winking, I add, "That's going to be my lead. And then I'll follow it with a line like: "Who is this man who speaks of understanding the present through history? He is Mr. Henry B. Frack, who is celebrating his thirtieth anniversary at WJB this year."

Derek speaks into his fist. "But, alas, he may be

131

the only person celebrating. Most of the students wish that instead of teaching history, Mr. Frack *was* history! Tadahh!"

We all laugh.

I look at my watch again. "Well, I guess it's time to call her. And then if you guys want to go over your articles, we could do that too."

"Great," Laura says. "Use the phone in the corner."

She points to a little table on the other side of the pool table. As I get up, Michael gets up from his chair, steps over the coffee table and sits down in my place. Next to Laura.

One small step for Michael, one giant step for womankind!

I take a deep breath and say shyly to Derek, "You want to come with me?"

I'm such an idiot. Where am I asking him to go? Across the stupid room.

But he grins as though I'd asked him to go to Paris. "Sure!"

As I dial, Derek watches. After one ring, Mrs. Garfield answers and I say hello.

"Well, hi, Molly. I've got the information."

"That's great," I say.

"When he was head of the social science research class, his kids won seven awards for history essays."

"Really?"

"Of course, that was twenty-five years ago." She laughs.

I guess Mrs. Garfield doesn't like Frack either.

132

"And, he's taught World History, Middle Eastern History, American History and American Foreign Policy."

"Thanks."

She laughs. "I use the word 'taught' in the loosest sense of the word, honey." Then, after a second, she asks about my mom.

Gosh. Everybody knows everything.

"Uh, she's better, Mrs. Garfield. Much better."

"Good. Would she be able to join us for Open School night? It might be fun."

"I'll ask her."

"Thanks, dear. Well, if there's anything else . . ."

That's when the idea pops into my hyperactive brain again.

"Uh, there was one other thing. Mrs. Marantz didn't have the exact date of the meeting, the board meeting when Mr. Frack switched to two classes a day. Do you remember when that was?"

There is silence on the phone. She'll never tell me. Never.

"I think it was three years ago last January. I'm pretty sure," she says.

Wow. I'm close.

"Thank you." Derek's eyes are starting to open extra wide. He takes my hand.

"Uh," I continue, "I have to say, when Mrs. Marantz told me the story of that meeting, you were great. You turned a defeat, you know, when he refused to retire, into a great victory by getting him to teach only two classes!"

133

"Why, thank you, dear," Mrs. Garfield says.

My heart is pounding. "No, Mrs. Garfield," I say, as Derek grasps my hand with his. "No," I say. "Thank *you*. Thank *you*!"

When I hang up, Derek opens his arms and wraps them around me. "Thatta girl!" he says. Then, leaning my head back, our eyes meet. And we kiss.

Then we kiss again.

After a few minutes, I look up to take a breath and to see Laura's reaction.

But she and Michael seem pretty busy too.

# Chapter 16

On Sunday, at exactly seven P.M., I turn on my computer to begin the article.

I would have started earlier, but this afternoon, my father forced the whole family to have a good time together again. He took all four of us to the movies to see one of my parents' favorite oldies, *Hair*. Luckily, we went to Glenwood, so no other kids saw us.

It actually was a great movie, but when my mom and dad walked into the lobby, they started to boogie.

Embarrassing.

Still, it was nice to see my mom happy. In the last two days, she's different every other minute.

Sometimes, she's attentive and loving, like when she told me Kathy called and asked me to call her back. I just couldn't do it, but my mom hugged me and said, "have a generous heart." I'm thinking about it.

Then, other times, just when I'm about to start gabbing, my mom is distracted again.

And this afternoon, when I finished the milk in the fridge and she had none left for her coffee, she was actually kind of snappy with me.

I understand that she's having a hard time. I really do. But I miss her.

Right now, I had better just concentrate on my article.

And Frack. And making the paper.

I'm excited and scared. I can't help fantasizing about what will happen once I write this.

Maybe Jeremy and Ms. Medina will love it.

Maybe they'll promote me right to the staff of the *Bugle*.

It's not impossible that a parent will read it and tell the real newspapers. Then Frack will resign. And then the *New York Times* will have a headline, "High School Reporter Topples Ineffectual Teacher."

Maybe *Sixty Minutes* will hear about it and come to our house and want to talk to me. And ask Billy what makes me tick. And make my mom so happy and proud that she'll forget her troubles.

That would be great.

On the other hand, maybe Frack will read it and get upset. Very upset. And then shoot himself.

Blow his brains out.

What if he did it in school?

Ugh.

Even though the man is pool fungus, I don't want him to commit suicide.

136

I'd feel guilty, even though he deserves this article. I'm just writing the truth.

If a kid who Frack flunked did himself in, Frack wouldn't care at all.

On the other hand, Frack's not me.

My fingers are beginning to cover the keys again when luckily, the phone rings. It's Derek.

"Hi," he says warmly. "Are you writing?"

"Yeah, but I can take a break. What's doing?" I ask.

"Well, I was talking to Karen Aaron . . ."

"You were? Why?"

"I called her."

"You did?" I ask, leaning back against my chair.

"Yeah. I know you're worried that there's not enough positive stuff about him. So I called Karen and asked why she liked him."

"Oh, Derek. That's brilliant!"

"I know," he answers and keeps going. "Anyway, here's the quote. Are you ready?"

"Uh . . . sure. Hold it. I'll type it right into my computer."

I type "Henry Frack—A Profile" by Molly Samantha Snyder. "Ready."

"This is it." Derek begins. "'Mr. Henry Frack has taught me more about the American Revolution and what it was really like to be alive in those times than I could ever know myself. He's a difficult teacher because he expects a lot from his students. This makes us expect a lot of ourselves. I will always be grateful I had a teacher like Mr. Henry Frack.' Karen Aaron."

"Wow. That's repulsively great. Thanks, Derek."

"Good luck!" he says. And hangs up.

I close my eyes, picture him kissing me again, and then get right back to work.

The first draft begins like this:

> *"We study history so that we may understand the past, so that we may better understand the present . . ."*

> *So says Mr. Henry Frack, history teacher at WJB. This year he is celebrating his thirtieth season as an educator. But who is this man who has influenced so many generations of WJB men and women? If we study Mr. Frack, perhaps by understanding him, we may better understand ourselves.*

> *Mr. Frack came to Bryan High School after completing a bachelor's degree (with honors) from Ohio State University. Soon afterwards, he was named head of the social science research project. It was during his tenure in that fine position that he brought home seven essay awards to WJB high.*

So far so good. I list all the courses he's taught over the years. Then I write:

> *Many students come to praise him. Karen Aaron, a student in his freshman class, for example, has said, "He's a difficult teacher because he expects a lot from his students. This makes us expect a lot of ourselves. I will always be grateful I had a teacher like Mr. Henry Frack."*

Based on what Derek's brother told me, I add a

138

line which is a slight distortion, just to make Frack seem like a better teacher.

*Charlie Anderson has said that many students keep his homework assignments years after they've completed his course.*

That's enough of the fluff. Now it's time for the heavy stuff.

*And yet he is also the subject of much controversy. Of the thirty current students this reporter spoke to, Ms. Aaron was the only one to praise him. A previous student, Dr. Judy Marantz, a psychology professor at Verona Community College, who studied with Frack almost twenty years ago, called him "incompetent and sadistic."*

That's a little strong. *Incompetent* is enough. I cross out *sadistic.*

*"He gave too much homework and he never taught," she went on to say. "He marked unfairly, and he read the grades out loud in class. He was a very upsetting and humiliating teacher to have."*

Hmm. It's hard to tone that down.

*A senior honor student who has asked that his name be withheld also accused Frack of arbitrary grading. "He never let us see our papers. If he didn't like you, you were doomed. I never received below a ninety at Bryan except for Frack. He failed me."*

Taking a deep breath, I keep writing, but the

more I write the angrier I get and the stronger the article gets. Finally, the last paragraph is finished.

> Dr. Marantz said "there's a Mr. Frack in every school. We all had someone like him. They may be troubled psychologically, or underpaid, or just burned out. It doesn't matter. It's important, as adults, to remember that they hurt our children."

> In the case of Mr. Frack, the faculty and PTA did try to do something. At a secret meeting four years ago, they asked him to retire. He refused. A compromise was reached in which he agreed to teach only two classes.

> ~~That is what he now does. This was a brilliant compromise, except for those fifty students who still face him every day.~~

> Note: Although Mr. Frack was asked to be interviewed for this article, he refused. His exact words to me were: "I don't have time for interviews."

After rereading once more, it still sounds very strong so I tone it down just a little more. The "note" goes.

But as soon as it's finished, bad fantasies start wiggling through my brain cells again like little worms.

Either Ms. Medina or Jeremy will hate it.

No. Worse. They won't hate it. They'll just like other articles better.

That's a real possibility and it makes me feel bad.

Getting up from the desk, I take a walk around

140

the house to calm down and then return to my room to rest on my bed.

It's not so terrible. I'll find another extracurricular activity.

Maybe I'll take up women's lacrosse.

No. You can get seriously hurt that way.

Maybe I'll ask my dad for violin lessons.

It would be great if I could learn to play the violin in two years and make the school orchestra. That would help get me into a good college.

Of course, being tone deaf would make that harder.

I clasp my hands and put them behind my head.

Who am I kidding?

Reporting is what I like. It's what I do best.

I have to give it my best shot.

I have no other choice.

And getting up, I go back to the computer and print out the article.

# Chapter 17

It's Monday morning at 8:30.

My lunchtime.

Standing outside the English office, I'm on the verge of handing in my opus. My exposé. My obituary. Suddenly I realize that it's crazy. It's too risky. I can't do it.

I'm not an investigative reporter. I'm not the star of *Sixty Minutes*. I'm just a kid.

They're going to hang me.

The headlines flash before my eyes: "Formerly Nice Girl Disappoints Everyone with Vicious Article."

I've never done anything that was this mean before.

At least—not intentionally.

Walking past the English office, and continuing along the third floor hallways, I peek into classrooms, thinking.

I worked so hard.

142

I tried my best.

I can't back out now.

If I don't hand this in I'll be worse than "not nice." I'll be a chicken.

Returning to the English office, I peek inside at the three empty desks and enter. A *Bugle* tryouts box sits on a corner desk. I kiss my paper, then gently toss it in.

As I'm walking out, Ms. Medina, coming in, bumps right into me.

"Sorry!" I say, embarrassed.

"What a way to go," she laughs. "Two Worlds Collide. Student and Teacher Knocked Unconscious!"

No wonder Medina's the *Bugle* adviser. She thinks in headlines too.

As I'm trying to get around her and out of the office, she takes my elbow. "Wait, Molly. Come and talk to me for a sec."

"Uh . . . well . . . sure."

I follow her to a desk. She takes off her dark green suit jacket to reveal a cream colored blouse with a big bow.

Ms. Medina looks a lot like my mom. Short. With a pixie haircut. Dimples. And a friendly face.

She puts the jacket on the back of her chair and smiles. "Well," she begins, sitting down. "I assume you just handed in your article."

"Yes," I swallow nervously. "Ms. Medina, when will we know if we were chosen?"

"I'll post a list during the day on Wednesday.

143

We'll be having another meeting Thursday afternoon for those who made it."

I nod and inadvertently sigh.

"Nervous?" She wheels her chair backwards toward the *Bugle* inbox. "I wish this weren't so competitive. I really do." Leaning over, she looks at the paper resting on top. Mine. "No matter what happens, Molly, you're a good English student. I like your writing."

"Thank you! Thanks a lot."

Peering at the title of my paper again, she shakes her head. "Frack, ay? You're the one who got Frack? I'm surprised he agreed to an interview."

I'm so nervous that I start curling the hair on the back of my head with my index finger.

"He . . . he didn't agree to an interview."

She looks at me, befuddled. "Then why didn't you come to me and get another assignment?"

I wrap the curl one way, then uncurl it the other way. "Uh, I thought of that but Jeremy said that since Frack's celebrating his thirtieth anniversary, the *Bugle* needed an article on him one way or the other. So I had this idea to write *about* him."

My finger is caught in the knot. I remove it gently with my other hand.

Ms. Medina studies me. "Well, fine. But then, why do you look so worried? Jeremy tells me you were editor of the Whitman *Wire* and you were a super reporter."

"Thanks."

Ms. Medina picks up my article. "You remind me of me when I was your age. I was one of those

144

kids who had the philosophy: "I am, therefore I worry!"

I laugh.

She sniffles. "Why are the best students the biggest worriers. Why don't the kids who should worry—worry?" She looks down at my pages. "I mean, how bad could this be?" she adds, chuckling.

"Hard to say, because, uh, I kind of did a stupid thing. I . . . I wrote the truth about Mr. Frack."

Ms. Medina squints with one eye, then the other.

I continue. "You know, the *truth*. As in 'the truth shall make you free.'"

Moving her chair forward, she puts her elbows on the desk.

"Go on."

"That's all. I did a lot of investigating and interviewing and wrote what I found out."

She takes the paper out of the box again. "I see. And I take it, it wasn't all flattering."

I curl a strand clockwise again. "Right."

Sitting straighter, she clasps her hands behind her head. "Well, it's silly to worry for nothing. Why don't you wait and I'll look at it now."

"You mean wait here? While you read it?"

She laughs. "Sorry. I wasn't thinking. Why don't you take a little walk around the hall and come back in ten minutes?"

So I do that. Even though my heart is pounding, I try to stroll calmly around the third floor, stopping at every bulletin board, reading every number or sign on every door. The halls are almost empty since most kids are in the middle of their first period class.

I keep trying to remind myself that it's no big deal. Either Medina likes my article or she doesn't like it.

If she likes it—great.

And if she doesn't like it—my life is over.

But I'll get over it.

After what feels like an hour, I'm back in front of the English office checking my watch.

Four minutes have gone by. I peek in the little window of the door. She's still reading.

Turning to the English bulletin board, I try to seriously consider what it has to offer. Should I spend the summer studying English literature in Peru? That would be good. Or should I go to summer school at Yale where, for many thousands of dollars, I can pretend I really go there. Or should I subscribe to *Time* magazine at the special student introductory rate of . . .

"Molly?"

Ms. Medina taps me on the back. I pivot around again. There is no expression on her face.

"Why don't you come inside?"

"Sure."

At her desk, we both sit down. Pulling the green jacket over her shoulders, she stares at me over little half glasses.

"Molly," she begins, "are you . . . kidding me?"

My jaw drops.

"Honey, what was on your mind? You know I

could never print this. You're so smart, why would you do this?"

I feel the tears in the back of my eyes, but I don't cry. "I . . . I don't know. I did it because . . . it was my assignment. And it's the truth. The more people I spoke to, the more I learned what a bad teacher Mr. Frack is. And always was. You don't know . . ."

"Yes, I do."

"Well then . . ."

Ms. Medina shakes her head. "Honey, I just can't print it."

My mouth won't open. Finally I whisper, "I spoke to lots of kids. I even left stuff out that was worse. And I said nice things too."

Ms. Medina shakes her head sadly. "We have a problem here. You know I'm on your side. I'd like you to make the paper. This isn't totally thorough research, but it does show courage. And it does capture the . . . unpopularity of the man."

I wrinkle my nose and try to be cute. "So what's the problem then?"

She smiles. "C'mon. You think Dr. Silverman, the principal, would ever allow this to be printed?"

I shrug. I feel tears welling up behind my eyes.

She puts her hand over mine. "Look, I know it's hard to have Frack. Believe me I do. My eldest daughter had him. And I had several blowouts with the man. But I don't agree with this Dr. Marantz. Sometimes, life isn't fair. And you just have to endure."

"I do understand that. I do, Ms. Medina," I say.

"But he was my assignment. And this is what I found out."

She taps the desk. "Let me think. Let me think. You don't have to do this but, I think I might have a compromise." She studies my article again. "As I say, this is nicely written. What if . . . what if you rewrite the first two pages a little bit."

"What do you mean?"

She hands me the article and I take a look at it again. On the first two pages are the good things I said about Frack.

"You can use the facts in those pages and just write a straightforward, informative background piece. Take out the compliments, so you're not writing what you don't feel, but give me a straight news piece. I know it's a compromise, but I could print it. And you would make the paper." She looks at me carefully.

I can't help it. I feel so confused. So disappointed.

"You mean forget all the other stuff?" I finally ask.

She nods. "Those are opinions. Yes, I'd like those out."

"Gee . . ." I feel like the breath has been taken out of me. "I was just trying to write an honest article about a bad teacher. You're always saying that literature should light up dark corners. Eliminate the lies. What about all that?"

"I believe that. I do. But there has to be balance here. And this is a student paper. It's just not realistic . . ."

I shake my head. "So, you're saying forget the truth. Is that it?"

148

"No. I'm not saying forget it. I'm saying there are many ways of handling the truth. But not this way. I honestly feel nothing would be accomplished by printing this . . ."

Suddenly, the sadness and disappointment I feel starts to turn to anger. I stand.

"Well, I don't feel that way, Ms. Medina. An article like this would accomplish something. It would make fifty kids who have Frack and who suffer every day feel better. They'd feel that the system let a kid express their side for a change. The system gave them a say." I feel the anger rising in my ears, and the passion coming to my voice. "I can't compromise. I can't! I'm willing to take a chance. I thought you of all people would too!" Then, turning toward the door, I can't help screaming my biggest insult. "And I heard you were at Woodstock!"

As I run out, bursting into tears, I slam the door behind me.

Which makes me feel pretty dramatic except for one thing. The door bounces right back open and I can't help looking back.

Ms. Medina is looking at me, a little shaken herself.

"I think you're wrong, Molly. I respect you a lot, but I think you're wrong. Why don't you take some time and think about my suggestion, okay? You have until Thursday. Because I'd like to have you on the *Bugle*."

And she gets up and closes the door.

# Chapter 18

"I think it's very flattering, Molly," my father says, as he passes the roast beef platter. "Very flattering that this teacher wants to work with you to get you on the paper."

The whole family is at the table. I put some meat on my plate and pass it to my mom.

"You should accept," my Dad continues. "Making the *Bugle* is a great start at Bryan."

"But, Dad, it's not that easy."

My mom passes a bowl filled with brussels sprouts to me. "It is very complimentary though, hon," she says softly. "I'm proud of you."

She seems to be in a pretty good mood right now.

I wonder if she'd get upset if I don't eat the brussels sprouts.

Just to be safe, I spoon up three of them and pass the bowl to Billy.

He tries to shift them casually to my dad, but my mom is watching every food pass at the table.

Billy looks up at her. "We had brussels sprouts for lunch at school," he says, with a dimpled smile. "Though these look excellent."

"They do," I agree diplomatically, even though the smell of brussels sprouts makes me turn brussels sprout green. Then, turning back to my father, I say. "Anyway, I can't decide what to do."

Billy cuts into his roast beef. "I'm a little surprised at Medina. She was my favorite teacher at Bryan. I thought she'd be more courageous. Gutsier. This is a cover-up."

My father frowns at him. "Young man, I appreciate your high standards, for Molly. But she's just being asked to write a factual piece. She has to be realistic. I think Ms. Medina is handling it rather well."

My mom points to the bowl. "Billy, try the brussels sprouts anyway. I made them a new way. With pecans."

Taking back the vegetable bowl reluctantly, Billy mutters, "The only way I like brussels sprouts is if they taste like green beans, Mom." But when she looks insulted, he puts some on his plate.

She smiles. Thank goodness. Encouraged, I ask for her opinion.

She puts her chin in her palm. "I don't know. I'm thinking."

My dad puts his palms up, like he's weighing justice. "Molly, I understand what you wanted to

151

do," he says. "But you could have wound up in serious trouble with that history teacher. And remember, being on the *Bugle* won't hurt your college chances. The better the college and your education, the better you can change the world later."

"I don't want to change the world later. I want to change it now! And I don't care if I would have gotten into trouble with Frack. He could flunk me anyway. Besides," my lips curl into a half smile, "most of our worries never happen."

My dad coughs.

"I believe in this, Dad. Where there's a will there's a way."

"Okay, okay." He puts his hand on mine. "I may have created a little monster here." He grins.

I turn to my mom again, figuring she should be finished thinking by now.

She makes a clicking sound in her cheek that means "this is a tough one," but begins. "You've definitely bumped into adult reality here, kiddo. And I'm not against compromise. It just has to be something you can live with. That's why I think you have to come up with your own answer."

"I know, and I will. But if you were me, what would your answer be?"

She takes the empty roast beef platter from the table and, walking over to the counter, puts it down. Turning around, she wipes her hands on her apron. "That's a good question, you know, I couldn't help thinking . . ." She studies me, then Billy, then my Dad.

152

"Go ahead, Mom," I say a little nervously.

She sits back down at the table. "Well, I couldn't help thinking about this book I'm reading that's helping me. It's about illness as a way of looking at everything, at any system. And maybe your situation isn't so different from . . . from mine."

"What do you mean?"

She swallows her food and then puts down her fork. "This book says that I'm . . . I'm a system. And I have something wrong with me. Like Bryan is a system with something wrong with it. Frack."

"Right."

"Well, according to this book, you can't pretend a problem's not there. The key question is, how do you face it in a way you can deal with, and make sure you survive? Do you know what I'm saying?"

I nod.

"It's hard. You're just a kid, over your head. You shouldn't have this problem. And," she shakes her head, "I wish I didn't have mine. But what we both need to figure out is what fight we want to make. Because I can understand that you have to fight Frack. Or anything. To make the system better. To feel better. To . . . survive."

She looks at me intently.

"I don't know." She shakes her head. "Maybe what I just said has nothing to do with your problem. I guess I'm just telling all of you how I feel."

She looks slowly around the table at each of us, and then speaks with determination. "I want to survive. I really do. I don't know the right answer for me either. And I'm scared . . . and the people I love are scared. But I'm going to take charge. I'm going to fight this, guys." She smiles shyly. "And I'm going to win!"

My father puts his hand out and takes hers.

And then Billy puts his hand over theirs.

And I put mine on too.

I wish we never had to let go.

# Chapter 19

I don't know what I'm going to do yet about Medina and the article, but in the spirit of facing things, I am standing on the Marantz porch.

I called Kathy back.

And she was really friendly and wanted me to come over and exchange clothes. She said she had lots of stuff for me.

She didn't even mention the mayor's party until I asked her and then she just said it was nice.

If she starts dropping names of rich and famous people, I'll ignore it. Or maybe I could tell her in a very nice way she's becoming shallow and inane.

Or maybe I'll just leave.

Maybe I should leave now.

No. I'm here in the spirit of compromise. And because my mom made another speech about having a generous heart.

I'll try to be generous. If she apologizes, I'll definitely forgive her.

I buzz the doorbell again and Princess comes bounding toward me. Kathy is right behind her.

As she opens the screen door, I take a deep breath, hoping to expand my heart, which constricts the minute I see her.

"Hi!" she says. "I'm really glad you came."

I smile semiwarmly and follow her into the kitchen.

She looks the same.

Although, her nose seems a little more turned up.

Nah. It's my imagination.

As soon as we get to the refrigerator, Princess nips at my shoe and pulls out my laces.

Kathy's about to grab her, but I shake my finger at the dog's nose, saying "No!" as firmly as possible. Princess drops the shoelace.

I did it. I'm definitely getting to be more assertive.

Today, Princess. Tomorrow, life.

Kathy puts her arm around me affectionately. "Good to see you. I'm glad you came." She gestures to the hall. "Let's go. I have so much stuff for you to look at."

"Great," I answer. "I brought a couple of things too."

And we bound up the stairs to her room.

I immediately hand her a green angora sweater which my mom got on sale and which is only slightly imperfect in the back.

"Nice." she says. "Don't you want it?"

I shake my head. "I look like Kermit the Frog in

it." When she laughs, I smile. I'm defrosting a tiny bit. "Anyway, I'm into tighter clothes."

"You are?" she says, opening her closet.

I shrug. "Well, I'm about to be. I hope."

We both study her closet floor. Picking up some royal blue iridescent stirrup pants from underneath the pile, she turns back to me. "What do you think?"

I shake my head. "Well, they're a tiny bit too tight. Just a tiny bit."

"Remember this, Molly?" In her hand is a fuchsia scoop neck top. "Remember when we went to that closeout with my mom and yours? We both begged for these." She winks. "We made such a fuss and now I never wear it."

I grin. "Me neither."

She turns back toward the closet. "Wait, wait, I see something." She pulls up her favorite and most beautiful tight red sweater from the floor. "You want this?"

"Don't you want it?" I ask. "That was your lucky sweater."

"Well, I'm a little tired of it. And I know you love it." She holds it up with two fingers. "Besides, I have a new lucky sweater. The one I met Nick in. Andrea thinks it's terrific too."

"Andrea?" I ask. "Who's that?"

"She's on the council with me. Remember I mentioned her. She's great."

I'm icing up again. I can't help it.

"Oh," I say, as she hands me the sweater. "Well, okay. Sure. I'll take it." Then, out of my mouth

157

pops, "If I can't wear it, I'll ask Laura if she wants it."

"Laura?" Kathy looks back at me.

"She and I are trying out for the *Bugle* together. She's terrific. We've gotten to be very close."

Kathy flinches just an inch. Good.

I can't help myself. I keep going. "Actually, we sort of have a crowd. Well, not a crowd, but a big bunch of kids. Well, not exactly a big bunch, but," I fumble for a second. "Four of us. It's really great. I love Bryan. It's so . . . unsnotty."

Kathy sits down on her bed. "That's nice," she says coolly.

We sit there silently for a minute.

Then our eyes meet. She looks hurt.

How can a person as nice as me, a person struggling with big issues like truth, justice and freedom of the press, be such a snit?

Easy. Kathy deserves it.

But I feel bad about it.

"Look, Kathy, I'm sorry. I said that stuff to make you feel bad. It's just that I never see you. And then last week, I know you got stuck but . . ."

She nods. "I know. I know."

I continue. "I don't even know Laura that well yet. I hope we become friends because I need friends at Bryan but . . . you've been so . . . not there for me. I was trying to hurt you."

She leans back against the wall and hugs her Grateful Dead pillow.

"It wasn't just that I was stuck last Wednesday, Moll." Her eyes meet mine.

158

"It wasn't?"

She shakes her head, which is hard since she's leaning against the wall. "I mean, I didn't know about your mom or I would have gotten there. Somehow. The truth was I wasn't stuck on Shore Boulevard. I was . . . I was mad at you."

I'm astonished. "Mad at *me*? Why?"

"Because. Because I thought you were only coming over to see my mom. You're so sarcastic about St. Bart's. And Nick. And my liking it there."

"Sarcastic? Me?" I ask.

"Yeah. 'Nick looks like the President of St. Bart's. I'm fitting in beautifully.' Those weren't compliments."

"Uh . . . true." She is so smart. I knew I used to like her for a reason.

"I just like St. Bart's a lot. And you'd get a kick out of some of this celebrity stuff too. I know what it is, and what it isn't, but I'm happy. I'm as happy as I've ever been."

"Okay! okay!"

She gives me one of those "see what I mean" looks.

Getting up, I walk over to Kathy's bureau and study her stuffed animal collection.

Then I turn around and look at her. "Maybe you're right. I guess I have been a little sarcastic. But I thought maybe you were turning into . . ."

She squints. "Into a St. Muffy's girl? No way. I mean, it's almost as though you didn't want me to be happy. My best friend."

I twist a stuffed giraffe's buttony eyes. "I do. I

159

do. I think. I mean I thought I wanted you to be happy at St. Bart's. But . . ."

She leans forward, her elbows on the throw pillow. "Yeah?"

This is embarrassing.

I stand the giraffe back up as I speak. "I guess I didn't want you to be *so* happy. So quickly. Without me."

She gets up and joins me at her bureau. "I figured. Well, I forgive you."

My mouth bunches into a pout. "On the other hand, you do seem impressed by St. Muffy–type stuff."

"Impressed, but not converted."

"And you should have called me after Wednesday."

"That's true. I called you Sunday. I wanted you to call me. And then my mom kept urging me. 'Call her again. Call her again.' So I got stuck arguing because she can be such a nag lately." She taps her teeth together. "But I should have. I really am sorry. And I'm sorry about your mom. Is she okay?"

"I don't know. I hope so. She's going back into the hospital Friday. She's having a lumpectomy. Which I think is good." I pick up some white harlequin sunglasses on Kathy's bureau and put them on to change the subject. "Anyway, I forgive you too."

"Good." Kathy studies me in the sunglasses. "Remember when we used to wear those and imitate Marilyn Monroe?"

"Sure." I hand the glasses over to her. "Go ahead."

160

She puts them on, and makes her lips quiver. "A lot of people think I'm just a sexy body," quiver quiver, "but I've got a mind too. And my mind is so thankful I have this sexy body."

I giggle.

Taking off the glasses, Kathy bites into one of the earpieces. "You know, speaking of mind, there's one bad thing about St. Bart's. It's hard. I'm . . . stupid there."

"No, you're not."

"Yeah. I am. I study my math for hours, but I don't understand one word. My mom thinks I'm lazy, but I'm trying."

"Maybe I could help."

She nods. "You're lucky, you're so smart."

I shake my head. "Kath, I have a twelve and a forty-four on my Latin quizzes so far, and I'm flunking history. And I'm not the smartest, not near the smartest in anything. Even in math. High school's hard."

"Really?"

I nod. "Wait'll my dad finds out I'm not a genius either. It's going to come as a shock."

She grins as I continue. "But you know what? I don't seem to care that much. I mean I care, but not that much."

Pushing away some dungarees, I sit down on Kathy's rag rug. "You know, it's funny. Before I came over, I had this feeling like it was up to me to be generous. I was thinking that I pretty much knew what was going to happen if we had it out. I'd say something, then you'd say something, then

I knew what I'd say, then what you'd say, then what I'd say and then I'd forgive you."

"It was hardly necessary to even come over. I appreciate it."

I grin. "Well, I wanted the clothes." We both burst out laughing.

"Isn't it amazing that life is a total surprise? Every day?" I say.

She nods.

I sit up. "I mean *every* day is a total surprise. It's like not one day is the same. Like no people are the same. Isn't that amazing?"

Kathy gets up and gets her Misty Rose nail polish from the bureau. She crosses her legs on the bed again, and begins to paint her nails.

"You know what's amazing to me?" she begins, painting her thumb.

"What?"

"What's amazing to me is that boys," she widens her eyes and begins to blush, "can sit down. You know what I mean?"

I start to grin. So does she.

Looking at me with total sincerity, she adds, "Especially on a fence. It's a miracle they don't hurt . . . themselves."

And I burst out laughing. Pretty soon we're both hysterical.

Gosh, I think. It sure is nice to talk about life with Kathy again.

I'm glad I came over with an open mind.

# Chapter 20

I'm staring at the English bulletin board again, waiting.

I peeked into the office five minutes ago, but Ms. Medina was talking to Jeremy about this afternoon's meeting.

Derek, Michael and Laura are going. They all made it. I was really happy for them.

A little jealous, but mostly happy.

Derek came over last night and we took a long walk.

He wished me luck. And he helped me. He said that even though I changed my mind thirty times, I wasn't wishy-washy. I was just, well, undecided.

His belching still bothers me a little, but I like him a lot.

On the other hand, I also know that if I made a list of the five most important things in his life, I don't think I'd be first.

First would be music. Or pool.

I might be second. Well, I might be tied for second with Nintendo video games.

As the door to the English office opens, and Jeremy walks out, I move from the wall. Jeremy turns toward Ms. Medina, puts a thumb up and walks past me.

Holding the door open to let me pass her, Ms. Medina gestures toward her desk. "C'mon on in, Molly."

I sit down catty-corner to her as she gets comfortable.

"Ms. Medina," I begin hesitantly.

"Molly," she interrupts, just as hesitantly.

I gather my courage and plunge ahead. "Ms. Medina, I've thought about this a lot. My brother says don't give in. My father says give in. My mom says I have to be me. And I say," I shrug, "she's right. And as me, I don't know what to do. I'm stuck."

Ms. Medina presses her fingertips together like a steeple. "You know, Molly, I've been thinking about you a lot too."

I squint. "Really?"

It's hard to believe a teacher thinks about students when they're out of sight. Even Ms. Medina.

She grins. "Yes, I have. I do think your article was inappropriate. I really do. One-sided. On the other hand, what it said happens to be, well, true. That's what I kept thinking about."

"Yeah."

She nods. "You know I try to make the *Bugle* a

paper to be proud of. But writing about a fellow teacher. And in that way. I was . . . taken aback."

"I wish, I wish we could come up with something," I say, "because I want to make the *Bugle* so badly. I want to compromise but not give up my principles altogether. Because I realize not giving up my principles is one of my most important principles."

Ms. Medina grins and hands me a lemon sourball. I take it and pop it in my mouth. As she talks, my mouth puckers.

"Well, I knew that," she begins. "That's why I started at Square One. The . . . situation . . . itself. Mr. Frack." She bites into her candy, and her lips pucker up too. "The thing is, over the last years the administration did try and failed to alter the situation. As you found out. But the faculty has just ignored it. We have so many other things to worry about in an overcrowded, understaffed school like this. You know, teachers aren't perfect."

"I know that," I try to say that without seeming sarcastic, but she grins.

"But your article made me remember that there are still fifty kids Frack teaches. They'll survive and all but, well, I decided to talk to some colleagues in the social studies department. And they started thinking too. And talking. And came up with an approach."

"Really? What do you mean?"

"Well, I'd rather not say. Let me just say that the

faculty, united, may have found a way to force a change. You might even see it this afternoon."

"Wow!"

I can't believe it. Maybe they found a way to fire him.

Or maybe just transfer him.

Maybe they moved him to the gym department.

I look at Medina for a second, but she doesn't say any more about Frack. "Now," she continues, "there's the matter of your article."

"Well, gee, this changes things. You're doing something! This is so great. I mean, whatever you did that's why I wrote the article!"

Ms. Medina smiles. "Exactly. So, can you rewrite the piece the way I suggested now?"

Leaning back in my chair, I take a deep breath. "I think so." My eyes widen. "Um . . . mostly."

She looks at me with narrowed eyes. "Mostly?"

I swallow, nervously. "Well, I could. I really could. Because this is so great. And I'm grateful. And happy. But," I crack into my lemon drop with my teeth, then try to tastefully pick the last bits from my molars, "but, well, I still feel uncomfortable." I move around in my chair. "Maybe I'll get over it." And I shrug. "I hope so."

Ms. Medina studies me. We sit for a minute.

Why can't I just write that article?

Then an idea comes to me. "You know, would it be okay . . . how about if maybe I just add one sentence that just says, in a very tasteful way, that Frack is controversial."

166

Ms. Medina's lemon drop goes from her left cheek to her right cheek. "Hmmm . . ."

"That way the article would be saying the truth." I look at her nervously. "That's the thing, you know, that the article should be true."

The lemon drop moves right to left again, and then Ms. Medina grabs it in the center with her teeth. A smile forms around it. "Clever. And good." She rolls the drop to the back of her mouth. "In other words, one sentence, that's honest, not malevolent, and very short!" She grins.

"I'll take it!"

"You got it!"

"Thanks, Ms. Medina."

Ms. Medina keeps nodding her head as she stands up. "I like it. In fact, it will make for a better piece." She shakes my hand. "You're tough, Molly! You're sweet, but you're also tough. I like that!"

I grin. "Thank you!"

"So I'll see you at the meeting," she says, as I stand up too.

"I'll be there!"

Medina stops as we reach the door and studies my face. "You know, Molly, you remind me of somebody . . . a boy I had two years ago. Your smile. You don't have a brother in this school, do you?"

I swallow. "Uh, I might."

"Very bright. Very perceptive."

"That wouldn't be my brother."

"Then you're not related to Billy Snyder?"

I'm surprised. "Yeah. But I could swear you said 'bright.'"

Ms. Medina laughs just as a boy rushes toward us.

"Isn't that him?"

Uh oh. It is.

When Billy reaches us, he shows Ms. Medina his dimples. "Hi, Ms. Medina. Remember me? I'm Billy Snyder."

She nods. "I know. In fact, my mind was just flashing on a term paper you wrote, about *The Scarlet Letter*. I think you called it "Better Red than Dead.""

Billy grins proudly, then looks at me questioningly.

She intercepts his glance with a grin. "Our meeting went very well. Molly will tell you all about it." She studies us. "Isn't that nice that you watch out for your sister. I wish my kids cared about each other that way. They just fight like cats and dogs. I'm going to tell them about you two."

Billy nods sympathetically. "Well, I find that if the older sibling is a superior person . . ."

I squeeze his waist with my thumb and forefinger. He tries not to grimace, but doubles over just a little.

"It's more a matter," I say, "if the younger person is patient because she realizes that the older sibling has probably regressed hopelessly since her birth."

Ms. Medina grins. "Right." She waves at both of

168

us with her index finger, and begins walking away from us. "Maybe I won't mention you two. See you this afternoon, Molly. And congratulations." To Billy, she adds. "You should be very proud of her."

My heart starts to skip a beat, because after a remark like that, my life would normally be in danger. But as Medina disappears from view, Billy doesn't give me a noogie, or even a wristburn. He just pats me on the back.

Hard.

Extremely hard.

But it's a step in the right direction.


It's five to two. I'm sitting in Frack's class, next to Derek, Michael and Laura, working on that "controversial" sentence.

Frack hasn't arrived yet.

I hope he isn't coming at all. I hope there's a new teacher.

When I told Billy that I may have caused Frack to be transferred or something, he was in awe.

I've never seen Billy in awe of me. It looked great on him.

He wanted to sneak into my class as a visiting foreign student, just to see what happened.

Thank God I talked him out of it.

It would be detention city—for both of us.

Derek nudges me and points to a sheet of paper. "How about this for the sentence," he says, reading. "Frack, a controversial teacher who disappeared mysteriously from Bryan last Thursday, will be sorely missed by some students. For the other four thousand kids at our school, however, there will be a humongous party in the auditorium!"

I giggle. "That's two sentences."

Derek winks. "Change that period in the middle to a semicolon."

Michael shakes his head. "Seriously, how about this? 'Because Mr. Frack uses modern teaching methods, in which the student learns by teaching him or herself, he is considered very controversial.'"

I look at him with admiration. "Excellent, Michael. Excellent. That's close."

We hear a stirring in the hall.

Everybody's pretty nervous. We can't figure out what the teachers have done. But kids have been coming up to me all period, congratulating me.

It feels great.

Derek smacks his lips. "Maybe we're going to get a new, young teacher. With a pulse. Maybe they're transferring Frack to some other class. I'd feel bad for those kids, but I'd get over it."

I shake my head. "Medina wouldn't do that. That doesn't solve anything."

Michael nods. "No, I think the teachers are trying to do the right thing. But what is it?"

Another kid, Nancy Wexler, turns around, and smiles at me too. "Congratulations, Molly."

"Thanks," I say modestly.

Inky Grant nudges me. "Molly," he whispers.

170

"Did you mention in the article that he destroys baseball cards and other valuable property."

I shake my head. "Uh uh, Inky."

He shrugs. "Well, if Frack's gone, losing Dwight Gooden will still be worth it."

I smile.

Just then the door opens and Mr. Rodriguez, the chairman of the social studies department, walks in and ambles to the back. He sits down.

Swiveling around in her seat, Laura takes a quick peek at him.

"Hmm," Michael whispers. "I wonder what he's doing here. Maybe he's going to introduce us to the new teacher!"

Derek gives him a punch. "I think you're right!"

Laura wrinkles her nose. "Hmmm," she says, "I have this horrible thought."

"What?"

She swivels in her chair again to study Rodriguez. "Couldn't be. Oh, it's too cruel. Too cruel."

"What?" I ask. "What?"

Just then, the door opens again. It's Frack.

I swallow nervously and whisper to Derek, "You think he's coming to say good-bye?"

Derek scowls. "I don't know. I don't think so."

Frack moves to his desk, waves to Rodriguez, and smiles a smile that looks a little unhappy.

"Good afternoon, class," he mumbles, putting down his briefcase, and rubbing his bald head. "I'd like to um . . . say something to the class about uh . . . some changes."

Changes. Wow.

More kids turn around to stare at me with admiration.

I feel pretty damn proud of myself.

I can't keep a grin off my face.

Laura nudges me. "I wouldn't smile so fast," she says.

Frack moves to the blackboard.

"Today, class, Mr. Rodriguez is our guest. And uh, several of the social studies teachers will be stopping by in the next few days. As my guests." He harumphs. "Therefore, today we will not be giving out any printed sheets."

Derek looks at me, still mystified, but pleased.

"And uh, I think we'll be cutting those committee meetings uh, short."

Laura groans. "Just as I thought, and all the teachers are in it together. That's why they're coming in every day."

I whisper back to her. "What? This is great so far."

"Instead," Frack continues, "today, and for the next few weeks, I am going to, uh, talk to you about the colonies. The life and customs of the people. Today, it will be the Virginia Colony. The World of Tobacco. I think you're going to find it fascinating."

Twenty kids turn around and stare at me, their mouths open.

Frack smiles as winningly as he can. "Let me begin by reading you a delightful passage by the Reverend John Clayton, who visited Virginia." He puts on his reading glasses, picks up a piece of paper and begins to drone.

"'And yet in truth 'tis only the barrenest parts that they have been cultivated, by tilling and planting only the highlands, leaving the richer vales . . .'"

My eyelids droop.

"'. . . when the cattle are weak, and venture too far after young grass.'" Frack looks up and smiles.

Inky Grant nods off, a low snore coming from his seat.

Michael and Laura groan softly.

"'. . . it will not bear tobacco past two or three years, unless cowpenned (and thus manured).'"

Oh my gosh. I get it now.

Leave it to teachers to come up with a sick solution to the Frack problem.

A very sick solution.

*They're making Frack teach.*

"Now, what is my point, class? What is my point?"

Laura nudges Inky awake, as all of us stare at each other, in shock. Derek belches. Laura keeps shaking her head. And Michael mutters, "Beware of what you want," as I try to figure out what I'm feeling.

Just then we hear a strange rumbling sound from the closet.

Mr. Frack hears it too.

He stops, listens, then walks over to the door and opens it.

Billy is standing against a bright red ski parka.

"Hi," he says, "interesting class. Very fascinating. Excuse me, I left my gloves here. Bye." And he begins to walk out of the closet.

He looks at Frack, who looks at Rodriguez just as Billy passes my desk.

"Way to go, dork . . ." he grins at me.

I frown.

But he laughs, and then whispers, "Really, it was still a great try. And this is soooo great! The man is teaching. So he's in pain."

And just as Billy pats me on the back and gives me a low five, we hear, "Hold it! Young man! Young lady . . ." It's Mr. Rodriguez and Mr. Frack, walking toward us.

"I don't know what's going on here," Mr. Rodriguez begins, "but unless you can explain this, it's detention for both of you!" He frowns as Billy tries to wipe the grin off his face. "I don't see anything funny about this situation," Rodriguez adds.

And then I can't help it.

And neither can the rest of the class.

Whenever a teacher says something's not funny, it results in just one thing.

We all start to giggle.